In The Shadow
Of The Swastika

A Sherlock Holmes Noir

J.G. Grimmer

Paperback ISBN 978-1-80424-734-1
ePub ISBN 978-1-80424-735-8
PDF ISBN 978-1-80424-736-5

Published by Orange Pip Books
An imprint of MX Publishing
335 Princess Park Manor, Royal Drive,
London, N11 3GX
www.mxpublishing.com

Cover design by Awan

"That was a right bloody cock-up, and no mistake." Sirens wailed past the building we hid in, panting, out of breath.

"Where are Watson and Mrs Hudson?"

"Haven't the foggiest. They're on their own," Sebastian Moran replied.

I nodded.

Moran rose to his feet "I'm not waiting. By now they're dead - or soon will be – by the hands of the Gestapo. See you in hell, Sherlock Holmes."

***

Seven days ago, Nazi London, 1936:

"Mycroft dies tonight."

Mrs Hudson and Watson applauded; the sound slamming off the rough bare concrete wall like bullets.

"To England." Mrs Hudson toasted, took an un-lady-like swig of whiskey and passed the bottle to me. It was throat-scalding good. I took another gulp. Then passed it to Watson.

To Edward VIII King, Wallis-Simpson Queen - Death To Tyrants.

***

Scotland Yard prepared to enforce the three p.m. until seven a.m. curfew as ordered by Dr Mabuse's SD Headquarters - Buckingham Palace.

A dozen black marias roared out of Police Headquarters Derby Gate, tires screeching. Wiggins chirped and the Baker Street Irregulars scattered like rats to disappear into the City's twisting alleys. Melting into one such labyrinth's shadows, Wiggins watched the Bedford wagons emblazoned with Prime Minister Oswald Mosley's British Union of Fascist's lightning S's.

A parade of bobbies followed, marching out of the gates in lock step, dressed in their dark blues and swastika armbands; the silver Death Head of the SS flashed, reflecting the cloud-shunned sun's feeble rays to spread throughout London.

Like cockroaches, Wiggins sneered, spat, and headed deeper into the alley. He didn't, wouldn't run.

In the first car sat Inspector Lestrade. His standing order from the Gestapo Black Book and SD Commander/London Dr Mabuse was the apprehension and arrest of Dr John Hamish Watson, Mrs Hudson, and myself along with all known associates, including the Baker Street Irregulars. Lestrade led the raid on our rooms at 221B Baker Street in the heady first days of the German Occupation.

TOO LATE, LESTRADE. AS ALWAYS.

He had kept, and now held tightly in his hand, the note I'd left him.

They tore through the place, searching for any clue as to our whereabouts, but to no avail. Not even a thimble of cigar ash was left. He ordered the building be put under twenty-four-hour surveillance until further notice.

The order stood for two years.

Lestrade knew his time was running out. If he didn't produce tangible results fast, there were plenty of sharks circling beneath his slowly leaking lifeboat, waiting to smell blood in the water - *his,* Gregson, chief among them.

"Stop the car," he shouted at the driver. "Back up and turn into the alley we just passed!"

"Right, Inspector!" The driver manoeuvred sharply into the alley.

"Available units block the Bond Street alley entrance," Lestrade shouted into the radio.

The driver positioned the wagon so close, the front bumper scraped against the two buildings, leaving a suspect no choice but to leap over the vehicle.

"Out! Sweep the alley!" Lestrade said, leaping out into the drizzle that just began to fall.

Three men joined him. Four others, their torches blazing in the shadowed gloom, approached from Bond Street.

Rain drops sparkled like diamonds in the beams methodically strafing left to right. Except for the sound of their hard-soled shoes striking the pavement there was no sound.

"Come out!" Lestrade said sharply. "Police!"

"I'll wager it was one of those so-called Baker Street Irregulars you spied, Inspector," PC Davenport said, scanning side to side. "Little buggers. Can't wait to have one strapped to a chair in Interrogation."

"They're the ones calling every hour clogging the switchboard; I'm sure of it; everyday with sightings of *Sherlock Holmes* here and *Sherlock Holmes* there. Can't get any bloody work done."

Before the two groups drew any nearer, Wiggins crouched and silently slipped through a narrow coal cellar window held open by Pilar. Torch beams and hunched shadows walked by. "Ogres," Pilar whispered, face smudged with soot. "In my home country, Romania, there are such creatures."

"They're just men here." Wiggins replied, snorting.

"Check every storm grate and window," Lestrade was yelling. *"Every one!"*

Circles of light approached the coal cellar window so fast, Wiggins and Pilar slammed against the wall so hard it took their breath away.

"Smythe, you better be certain." Lestrade's voice could be heard clearly. His and the other man's features were rendered indistinct blurs by the filthy window.

"This window hasn't been opened in months, perhaps years, Inspector."

"Right, move on to the next! We haven't all day!"

It wasn't until the sound of auto doors slamming and engines roaring into the distance that Wiggins and Pilar risked taking a breath.

"You're right, *definitely* ogres."

The little Gypsy girl smiled.

"We'll wait a little longer, make sure they're gone. All right?"

The cramped room suddenly filled with light and the smell of boiled cabbage.

"Ere?! What're you doin in my house?!" A fat shadow roared; man or woman, Wiggins couldn't tell. As he moved toward it, the door slammed shut. "I'm callin' the p'lice," the muffled voice cried, as the bolt was slid into place.

"Out you go, little one!" Wiggins urged, opening the window, and lifting Pilar. "I'm right behind you!"

Once out, the two ran in opposite directions as police sirens grew louder.

***

I bellowed with laughter as Wiggins and Pilar relayed their outing. "Marvelous!"

"Oh, you poor dear," Mrs Hudson said, fussing over Pilar with a wet towel, then directing her death stare toward Wiggins. "What were you thinking, stuffing this little girl into a coal cellar? Don't worry dearie, I'll soon set you to rights."

The little girl tried to bat the towel away from her face.

"Leave her be, Mrs Hudson," I said. "I wish I'd been there to see the look on Lestrade's face – outwitted again. Well done! You are both a credit to the Baker Street Irregulars."

"Best get some rest, now," Watson suggested.

"What do you mean, Doctor?" Wiggins exclaimed. "There's work to do!"

Pilar nodded emphatically. "That's right, we're set to meet up with Simpson and the others later; they've been tracking Mr Mycroft's movements all day, isn't that right, Mr Holmes?"

"Quite right," I replied. "No time to lose, Watson. England has been under the boot of traitors far too long. It ends now."

Watson said nothing. Since Mary's execution, he'd changed – and not for the better.

I feared it was all my fault.

"Off you go," I said, shaking off the thoughts.

Wiggins and Pilar smiled wide and scampered off.

"What a touching display," said a voice from the shadows. "I was moved, you know."

Professor James Moriarty materialised in front of us.

Mrs Hudson shrieked. "Stop doing that, you horrible man!"

The Napoleon of Crime regarded her, his clean-shaven face slowly oscillating from side to side in a curiously reptilian fashion, which did nothing to put Mrs Hudson at her ease.

"My apologies, Mrs Hudson. I have always been… *quiet*."

"Presumably you've come to present your report, Professor." I said, lighting my briar.

Our eyes locked, and a wave of palpable, living hatred rippled through the air, dissipating as quickly as it had come. It happened each and every time we were in close proximity. Somehow, in those few seconds, our intellects triumphed over our primal egos and we managed not to kill each other.

"My report is, as always, Minister of the Realm Mycroft Holmes is too well protected, and too nimble in his thinking to ever be caught off guard."

I raised my eyebrow at him, ignoring his thinly veiled *"especially by you"* insult.

Moriarty sighed and continued. "Colonel Moran has secured a sniper's perch as well as enlisting the participation of other assassins who have chosen their own firing positions."

Closing my eyes, I returned my attention to my pipe.

My nemesis retreated to the shadows.

***

Inspector Lestrade returned, dripping wet and short-tempered, to his office following a fruitless two-hour long sweep from the East to the West End, to discover a truly unexpected visitor. His right arm shot out in salute as his heels clicked together.

"Minister of the Realm. What can I do for you, sir?"

8

Mycroft sat in the widest chair available, languidly puffing a large cigar, flanked by two steely-eyed men in black suits.

"Nothing," he said quietly, face disappearing behind a thick cloud of smoke. "Unless you are about to present me with my brother's head on a platter, or inform me that he is in the hands of your most thorough interrogators."

"Sir, I—"

"Out with it, man!" Mycroft's voice boomed like thunder from the cigar smoke that still obscured his face. "You've had two years. *Two years!* With the most efficient and ruthless secret police resources in history at your disposal!" He rose like a mountain come to life to stand toe-to-toe with the Yard's Chief Inspector. "Now you have two days! Or it will be *your head!"*

Lestrade held himself ramrod straight and didn't breathe until long after the Minister of the Realm left, the stinking cloud of cigar smoke trailing behind his expansive posterior. *Didn't cigars go out of fashion when they strung Churchill up,* he thought.

"Carstairs, increase the round ups," he barked into the phone.

***

"After Mycroft, then Mabuse, Chamberlain, Halifax – one by one until the entire Cabinet is dead!"

I paced smoke billowing furiously from my pipe.

"Then the pretenders to the throne!" Mrs Hudson said hotly, heart hardened by the many public executions she'd witnessed. "In revenge for all the people lined up and shot on Baker Street, just below your window. They too must die!"

"Mrs Hudson is right," Watson added. "England may have been taken without a shot, thanks to the traitors within, but no more! We must stop the forced deportations, the middle-of-the-night arrests, all of it."

"No more indeed." I stopped pacing and grinned like Incarnate Death. I directed their attention to the tilting table and the map of London I unfolded marked by Xs, each accompanied by the drawing of a bullet.

Mrs Hudson and Watson exchanged a glance.

"Colonel Moran and his hand-picked gunmen aren't the only ones marking targets. I've been laying my own traps."

Watson looked closely, but could make neither head nor tail of the dizzying array of symbols, letters, and numbers appearing next to each X and each bullet.

"It's best if you do not understand." I told him. "Make no mistake; you have a role to play, as do you, Mrs Hudson."

"Well, that's all right then," she huffed, and walked off.

***

Dusk draped itself around London like a burial shroud as I rose like a revenant from deep beneath the London Necropolis Railway Station. Opened in 1854, it transported both mourners and the deceased directly from Central London to Brookwood Cemetery in Surrey until it was shut down by the English Nazis in 1935.

It is one of many refuges we use, changing locales frequently.

A group of a dozen young men and women dressed in evening clothes sauntered past laughing, yelling, and passing a flask.

Bright Young Things, scions of Britain's aristocratic elite who ignored curfews and against whom the law turned a blind eye. After all, it was their parents who welcomed the Nazis with open arms, souls bought and paid for – just like the rest of us.

I followed the pack at a discreet distance, focused on two young men walking arm in arm. I'd been stalking them for the past fortnight, certain they'd been murdering any homeless person they came across. Thus far, seven street people had been butchered, their deaths going unmentioned in the two approved State newspapers; Viscount Rothemere's Daily Mail and Daily Mirror.

Rothemere, or Harold Harmsworth, was one of the key people in ushering in England's New Dark Ages; a simpering, feckless Hitler enthusiast who believed fascism is the future, the foundation of a new order that would replace parliamentary democracy and self-determination (and whose name appeared on my map of Xs and bullets).

The pack entered a brightly lit nightclub, loud music cascading from the open etched-glass doors to cruelly fill the deserted street with the illusion of gaiety. I backed into the shadow of a doorway, prepared for a long night. I smiled when I met my own eyes staring back – my face on a wanted poster plastered to a streetlight:

WANTED: SHERLOCK HOLMES

A Reward Will Be Presented To The Citizen Who Leads The Police To Him

The State Needs You!

Do Your Part!

In smaller letters below, it read: *"Contact your local Vigilance Committee with any and all information regarding the whereabouts of this Enemy of The State and People. By Order of The Minister Of The Realm."*

I'm going to enjoy watching you die, Mycroft, I thought, salivating.

Riotous laughter spilled into the street along with half the pack. I scanned the faces, but did not see the killers of the homeless. Quickly and quietly, I sped to the alley behind the club, but saw no one; except for the band and employees, it was empty. Feeling exposed, I hugged the wall and moved away.

Four shadows blocked my path.

"What have we here?" One of them asked, her cultured accent tainted with cruelty.

"Told you we were being followed."

"Did you get him?"

They were joined by more, their voices behind me.

"We did."

Bloody hell, I thought.

The back of my head exploded in light and pain. I fell into darkness…

When I came to, a thick German accent rumbled through my head like the drumbeat of a Nazi rally.

"So, the great Sherlock Holmes. I must admit I am disappointed."

"Not as much as I am in myself. Kill me and be done with it."

"Kill you? I'm not going to kill you, Herr Holmes. I saved your life!"

Finally, I was able to open my eyes. Swirling nauseatingly into focus was a round face with a cigar in a holder stuck in its mouth. This man helped me to sit up and poured tepid water down my throat.

"Inspector Karl Lohmann, Kripo. I found you on your face in the alley and brought you to my room."

Regaining my senses after coughing up most of the water I asked, "Kripo? What is a Berlin detective doing in London?"

I looked around the dinghy room; there were faded paintings, peeling wallpaper, and the odour of mould. So, not the Grosvenor. Interesting.

"Taking in the sights, of course," Lohmann laughed, then as if a switch was thrown, deadly serious, "I was following those delinquents too."

"Why?"

"They are not, how do you say, Ordinary."

"Oh? How so?"

He took several long drags of his cigar. "They are the children of Mabuse."

"Enlighten me, Inspector."

"It is quite simple," he said, eyebrows raised as if I were a doltish pupil. "They do his bidding."

"If by that you mean they are committed Nazis I would…"

"No, no, no! Mabuse has control over them, body and mind! What he wills, they do. The murders of those street vagabonds is only one example. Didn't you see their *eyes?*"

I sighed, wincing at the pain searing the back of my head.

"You do not believe me?"

"The fact that I'm sitting here with you and not this moment having my manhood skewered by hot needles negates your interpretation of the facts."

He stood up straight. "Herr Holmes, you are an imbecile."

"Undoubtedly." I grinned sardonically.

"I have pursued Dr Mabuse since the Twenties. He is not human."

"Neither are the Nazis. Just how did you save my life, Herr Lohmann?" I moved too fast. A wave of vertigo crashed over me. Gritting my teeth I clutched the wall like a gecko, hoping not to fall on my face.

"It's *Inspector* Lohmann," he said, foul breath moist on my face, while roughly depositing me on a chair. "And as I said, I was following the group you were. Unlike you, I can go where I please, being German *and* a policeman. While you were shivering in the damp, I was warm in the club. When they split up, I followed those who went out to the alley. I overheard them saying they were being followed."

"They couldn't have known that."

"But *they* did, Herr Holmes."

"Because they are in the thrall of Dr Mabuse?"

"Precisely!" Lohmann stabbed the end of his holder at me like a knife.

"And then?"

"I watched them corner you but held back."

"Most kind."

"Nothing personal. I stepped forward when the young lady's blackjack cracked your skull and she kicked you in the ribs."

"And they just walked away?"

"Of course not. I flashed my warrant disc, and told them to piss off."

"I see."

"What are you looking at?"

"The deep red indentations either side of your nose, Inspector."

Lohmann produced a pair of black glasses. "For protection."

"From the sun? Because you won't find much of that in England. Those, however, are made to protect welders."

"No. Protection from Mabuse and his minions."

"Is that why you're staying in this rat-hole?"

"I'm working undercover."

"If Mabuse sees you as an enemy, I understand."

"He doesn't. Soon, he will pay for underestimating me."

I didn't doubt his resolve, but the mind-control mumbo jumbo? Rubbish!

I walked into the night on unsteady feet, seeing double.

***

Though I was invisible in the shadows, a sleek coupe paced me.

"You'd better get in. You look like you're about to fall flat on your face."

Insufferable woman. I waved her on.

"Suit yourself," Irene Adler huffed. "But you're being tailed."

I sighed and did as I was told.

"That's a fine way to thank me," she said as we accelerated down the street.

"You do know there's a curfew."

"A girl's got things to do. Besides, I've got a few connections at Scotland Yard. Lucky for you, I was passing by. You look like hell"

I grimaced.

Irene lit a cigarette and passed it to me. "There's a flask in the glove compartment."

I took a whiff and tentative swig. It was good. I took more.

"Hey, easy with that! You've got a head injury!"

I finished it off. Adler's voice faded from annoying mumble, to irritating whisper, to…

"*Wake up!*"

My gummed-sealed eyes opened; it was touch and go if they ever would.

"Do you want to die!?"

"No wonder you live alone," I mumbled, gingerly touching the dressing taped to the back of my head. "Or your neighbours are deaf."

"Shut up and sit up!"

"How did you get me in here? A friend from Scotland Yard?"

"No, but with the reward on your head, you've given me an idea. Maybe another time. Now on your feet. I don't know if you have a concussion." She grabbed me roughly under my shoulders. "One foot in front of the other."

"Shrew," I muttered, shuffling along.

"What did you say?"

I filled and lit my pipe instead of answering. "You said someone was tailing me."

"Yes."

"Did you get a look at him?"

"Why does it always have to be *a him?*"

"Was it *a her?*"

"I couldn't tell. It was a tall, thin figure wearing black – a trenchcoat, I think."

"I'm feeling much better, thanks. See you around." I said and grabbed my coat.

"Be careful."

I was.

I'd never take Adler into my confidence again, since it was because of *her* that Mary Watson died.

***

"Elliot didn't show for our meeting, so I went over there." Wiggins said, face white as a sheet. "When I got there, his da's tailor shop was tore up like by some wild animal – and the blood. There was so much of it, sprayed on the walls, the floor… It was everywhere. But of Elliot, and his parents, not a sign."

"What else?"

He blinked at me.

"What else did you observe?" I repeated.

"The neighbours." Wiggins replied, colour slowly returning to his cheeks.

"What about them?"

"'Bout their business, like nothin' happened."

"The rest of Brick Lane?"

"Same. Nobody heard nothin'."

"And Mycroft?"

"Except for a visit with Lestrade, he hasn't moved from the Diogenes."

"Thank you, Wiggins."

"Mr Holmes, the Irregulars are keeping tabs on Elliot's place, quiet-like."

"Good job Keep me informed."

"Yes, thank you, sir." Wiggins left after Mrs Hudson forced a bag of food on him.

"Shouldn't you go and have a look at Elliot's place for yourself?" Watson asked.

"No."

His eyes sparked. "A trap?"

"Likely. The Irregulars will inform me how heavy handed Lestrade or the Gestapo are with their presence. The fact the residents act as though nothing happened indicates as much."

"Then little Elliot and his parents may be alright?"

"They may have even escaped, their shop ransacked and staged for my benefit."

"Monsters."

"Monsters, indeed,." I replied. The biggest being Mycroft. "Care to join me in a pipe, Watson?"

"Way ahead of you." Watson said, lighting his.

Neither of us spoke another word. Each lost in his own thoughts. Mine were filled with Mary's loss.

When all was quiet, I slipped into the night. Headache be damned. Just before dawn I came across a body on the Embankment. Only this wasn't a street person, but a policeman. His throat had been slit from ear to ear and he bled out white and quickly. I relieved him of his notebook and beat a hasty retreat.

**

Inspector Lestrade knelt in a puddle near the murdered officer, water and blood seeping through the knee of his trousers. Both ends of the Victoria Embankment were blocked by Metropolitan Police and uniformed members of the SS. There was a growing group of Reich citizens curious to see what all the fuss was about.

"PC No 931's patrol log is gone, Inspector," Detective Sergeant Hawthorn reported.

"Wallet? Jewelry? Do you know him?"

"All here, Inspector. His name's Evans, I think."

So, a political killing, Lestrade thought, *the Gestapo are going to have a field day*. More round-ups. More reprisals. He examined the body himself after spotting Beckert coming through the police line.

"You're on report, Hawthorn. What's this?"

The officer looked at the dead man's hand. "What's what?"

"Yes," Beckert whispered menacingly. "What's what?"

Hawthorn snapped to attention in the presence of the Gestapo operative.

"One of our officers was killed, Major Beckert." Lestrade said evenly. "And robbed. His ring is gone. I was showing Detective Sergeant Hawthorn the difference in coloration on the finger. You see, Hawthorn, the flesh holds the ring's outline."

"Yes, sir," Hawthorn replied, looking carefully. "Thank you, sir."

Beckert tipped his black fedora forward, silver death head ring on display. He smiled unpleasantly, his clean-shaven face, round like the moon, his protruding eyes aglow. "Forgive me, Inspector, I find your theory that this murder was a simple robbery to be unconvincing. Perhaps your dead officer simply forgot to put it on or lost it?"

Lestrade nodded tightly. Beckert gave him the creeps.

The Gestapo agent flashed his warrant disc for all to see. "This murder is political and is now a Reich security matter. Detective Sergeant Hawthorn you will be seconded to this investigation."

Standing among the onlookers, Beckert spied Spoerri, Mabuse's manservant, watching him. He was always watched by Mabuse.

Hawthorn saluted, grinning smugly, basking in the glow of Nazi recognition.

Imbecile, Lestrade thought and waved the coroner over to examine the body.

"Major," Hawthorn said, "his patrol notebook was also taken."

"Oh?" Beckert said, looking too closely ,too avidly at the officer's slit throat. "I wonder why you didn't divulge that bit of information, Inspector."

Lestrade said nothing.

"What do you think, Michaels?" Beckert went on. "The blade work is professional?"

Dr Michaels, the corpulent coroner nodded. "Yes. Very neat, the hand very sure."

"So, you would conclude that this was a political assassination?"

"Oh, undoubtedly, Major Beckert."

"Thank you, you may take the body. Inspector Lestrade, you are of no further use here."

Pressing his lips tightly together, Lestrade clicked his heels, saluted smartly and strode to his car.

Beckert waved over an SS corporal and whispered in his ear.

"Englanders! Over here now," the corporal snarled.

The crowd of a dozen, mostly factory workers, local shop owners, and office clerks were roughly rounded up and funneled single-file to stand frightened and pale before Major Beckert, who silently held out his black-gloved hand. He examined their identity papers carefully, whistling "In the Hall of the Mountain King" by Grieg, wearing a superior smirk.

Afterward, all were arrested, shackled, and shoved into a police van.

Detective Sergeant Hawthorn got into Beckert's sedan.

I watched the scene with bated breath, anticipating the moment I could cut Major Beckert's smile off his face. The familiar pungent aroma of a cheap German cigar billowed around me as a beefy hand lit on my shoulder.

"Good to see you again, Mein Herr!"

"And you as well," I replied to the broadly smiling face of Inspector Lohmann.

"Let's go somewhere quiet, and I will tell you about Major Hans Beckert."

We took seats at a dirty café.

"May I see your papers?" he whispered conspiratorially.

I slid them across the splintered table-top beneath my palm.

"These are very good," he declared, sliding them back to me. "I doubt they'd be questioned even by Beckert."

I raised my eyebrow expectantly.

We were served pale watered down tea in filthy cups without saucers.

"He was a child-killer in Berlin that I had caught in 1931. Probably still is."

For appearances, I took a small sip of the cold urine-coloured liquid that was not worthy to be called tea. "Let me guess. Another case of yours? Splendid."

Lohmann's face reddened. "He had friends in the Nazi Party."

"Had?"

"Has. It was a Nazi judge who dismissed his case."

"Even then?"

"Even then, the Nazis had infiltrated nearly every walk of life."

I shrugged. "He'll neither be the first, nor the last psychopath to become a Nazi. From what I've observed."

"For the record," Lohmann said, lighting a cigar. "I am *not* a Nazi."

"*That* I have observed, Inspector."

"How's your head?"

I grimaced more than smiled. "No permanent damage. Thanks for asking."

Everything about the Berlin detective was rumpled; suitcoat stained and wrinkled, shoes scuffed beyond repair; but he possessed an ordered mind, and I had no doubt that, despite his difficulties with Mabuse and Beckert, he was a competent investigator.

"There was another murder of street people last night." Lohmann said, drawing on his cigar. "A short distance from that club. It was monstrous, like your 'Jack the Ripper.'"

"Man or woman?"

"An entire family. Butchered like pigs. I watched the bodies being carried out, blood dripping down white arms dangling from the side of the gurney, sheets covering the bodies soaked red. It reminded me of the trenches."

Lohmann mopped the sweat beading on his face with a yellowed handkerchief.

A chill slashed deep and cold into the marrow of my bones like a cut throat razor.

"On Brick Lane?"

The German squinted at me through the smoke of his cigar. "No, I do not recall the name, but I'm certain that was not it. Why?"

"Confirming a theory."

The Inspector's penetrating gaze, the furrowing of his brow, conveyed his skepticism.

"Perhaps one day you'll share it with me."

"Perhaps."

"More tea?"

I blinked at him. He smiled. Realisation dawned.

"You knew Beckert had been assigned to London. You're after Mabuse *and* him, aren't you?"

Lohmann didn't speak, but he didn't need to. I recognised the darkness in his eyes; I saw it every day in my own.

***

Understanding one was under constant surveillance in theory was quite different to reality.

"You startled me!" Mycroft exclaimed to the lithe thin silhouette standing in the corner who bowed stiffly then moved with the grace of a dancer to stand in front of the expansive oak desk in the office of the Minister of the Realm-GB Nazi Reich, formerly known as the exclusive gentlemen's club, The Diogenes. The figure was dressed all in black, the pale waxwork face expressionless like the sphinx, gaunt like a skull, intentions unknowable behind black spectacles.

Mycroft thought the figure as an *it,* not a *he*, for it was not a man at all.

More the shell of one.

Possibly a wraith. Certainly soulless.

It stood motionless, then tiny pinpricks of light appeared like stars in the centre of the dark glasses. When it spoke, the voice of Dr Mabuse issued from the slightly parted lips. "My patience is at an end, Realm Minister Holmes. You have one day to bring me the heads of Sherlock Holmes and Dr Watson. Or yours is forfeit."

"Yes, Herr Doctor!" Mycroft said, right arm shooting out in salute, then bowed. When he looked up the pale man was gone without a sound. He picked up the phone.

"I want every building, I repeat *every building,* searched. London must be turned upside down! Mobilise Special Branch, Scotland Yard, City Police, the SS, and Gestapo!"

"Yes, Minister." His secretary replied.

"Room by room, the Tube, sewers, *every* place the traitor Sherlock and his accomplices could possibly crawl into!"

Stevens, the Realm Minister's most trusted servant, entered Mycroft's presence, slightly out of breath. He'd been tasked with following the wraith.

"Well?"

"Sorry sir, I lost him."

"Have you at least been able to identify our silent friend?"

Stevens smoothed his pencil moustache. "The nearest I've been able to place him is in the German town of Holstenwall."

"I've never heard of it."

"Few people have, sir. In fact, it doesn't appear on any map I've looked at."

"What did you find out about him?"

"It is very fragmentary, Realm Minister, but I've gathered that a person of his description was involved in a series of murders; though of *whom* precisely have been lost. A great fire destroyed the town's records."

"How convenient."

"Indeed, sir."

"I've ordered a City-wide house-to-house, room-by-room search for my traitor brother. This will last for twenty-four hours, or until he is found and arrested."

"Yes, sir."

"You will coordinate with Lestrade and Beckert. Keep me informed every step of the way."

"Of course, sir."

"Find him fast. Dr Mabuse has given me twenty-four hours to keep my head."

***

The full weight of the English Nazi jackboot fell on London like the hammer of the gods. The contents of entire apartment buildings, hotels, and homes were turned out into the street. Rain or shine, the SS, Gestapo, and City police swung their clubs and truncheons, setting their vicious dogs on any person foolish enough to stand in their way.

Watson, Mrs Hudson and I barely kept ahead of the juggernaut. In fact, we were down to two choices; turn ourselves in, or live under the waters of the Thames, breathing through straws.

"Or you could stay with me," Inspector Lohmann said. "My hovel was turned upside-down and inside-out early this morning. They've moved on."

Hovel was the most generous description of Lohmann's abode possible, as well as being a bald-faced lie. There was barely room for one person, let alone four, and tempers grew very short.

"Being strung up with piano wire by my thumbs would be preferable to your stink," Watson bit out.

"And must you smoke those foul cigars in here?" Mrs Hudson asked. "There aren't any windows to open!"

I sat wedged into the corner, eyes closed.

"This is the gratitude I get for opening my home to fugitives!"

"*Home?*" Watson exclaimed. "This is a cupboard! Of a child's dollhouse!"

"What Dr Watson and Mrs Hudson are trying to say under these trying circumstances is thank you, Inspector Lohmann."

Smiling gregariously while expelling a vast cloud of cigar smoke to mingle with the greenish grey fug that perpetually hung in the air, the Inspector laughed. "Schnapps anyone?!"

Soon we found the claustrophobic closeness didn't trouble us as much as we thought.

***

Major Hans Beckert sauntered into the interrogation room whistling the same tune. Children were shackled to their chairs, which in turn were bolted to the floor. He stopped for a moment in front of each, the smile on his lips never reaching his dead eyes. There were five in all: four boys and one girl.

"And what is your name, child?" The nasty man asked, his face inches from the girl's.

Neither she, nor the others spoke.

"Detective Sergeant Hawthorn! Identify these vermin," Beckert shouted, voice breaking.

"I don't know them, sir!"

Beckert straightened and spun around, hand lashing out to strike Hawthorn's face hard. "Idiot! Are they the so-called Irregulars you spoke of or are they not?!"

Hawthorn stood to attention, his right cheek glowing red. "They are, Major! But I do not know their names. Sir!"

Beckert smoothed down his black hair, parted in the Hitler style. "Everyone out!"

Once the room was clear, he turned back to the children, focusing on the youngest. "When I return, each of you will tell me your name, your parents' names, address if any, and where the traitor Sherlock Holmes can be found. I trust you're afraid of the dark. And if not, you soon will be! Lights out!"

He giggled menacingly as the heavy door slammed shut.

The darkness was total.

"What bollocks," Wiggins muttered and yawned loudly.

Simpson, Ozzie, Rohan, and Pilar snickered.

Screaming erupted all around them.

"What is that?"

"It's all right, Ozzie," Wiggins said soothingly. "Just a trick."

The sound of metal sliding on metal echoed sharply, followed by squealing.

"Ah," Rohan wailed, crying. "Rats! Rats!"

"Stomp your feet," Wiggins yelled. "That'll keep the buggers off ya!"

***

The entire City of London was shaken to its prehistoric foundations for a full day and night, as the SS, the Gestapo, and their lackeys in Scotland Yard and City Police searched for us. It was thorough if nothing else. Mycroft must have had his worthless life threatened from on high to mount such an operation, little good it would do a dead man.

His death was preordained, no matter what happened to me.

The door swung open so hard it tore away from its hinges as Lohmann burst in. "Get out! The Gestapo are on their way!"

His shouting did nothing for our hangovers, except make them worse. Mrs Hudson went one way, Dr Watson the other, while I did likewise.

"It was my landlord," Lohmann whispered as I reached the door.

"He'll be dealt with," I replied. "You'd better come with us."

"I know the place. Thank you."

***

Two streets over, Mrs Hudson approached a checkpoint and confidently thrust her papers in the face of a young constable. "Be quick, young man. I have my duties to tend to."

"Yes, mum." His eyes flicked from the picture on her I.D. to her face. "Your papers are in order, you may pass."

He was so young, he probably didn't even need to shave. Squaring her shoulders and nodding tightly, Mrs Hudson bustled past. Once out of sight she turned down a narrow cobblestone alley, then another, and another. Finally able to let down her guard, she despaired for the boy.

Soon he'd be old enough to be sent to fight for the Nazis.

And die in some far off land.

Cannon fodder for Hitler.

***

In the relative safety of a tenement doorway, Dr Watson adeptly applied a pair of very bushy white eyebrows and even bushier moustache, a felt hat, rimless spectacles, and finally the Gold Party pin signifying Elder Member status in the British Union of Fascists to his lapel. Adopting the arrogant carriage of one of the privileged Elite, he marched down the street as though he owned it, going so far as to ignore the tenants of a building that had been thrown out of their homes while SS and Gestapo men could be heard ransacking them.

One of the guards spotted Watson's pin and came over to him. "Sir, allow me to escort you from here. For your safety."

Watson glared at him. "Don't you have them under control, Sergeant?"

The man paled and blushed at the same time. "Why, of course, sir... I—"

"Then do your duty. If I ever see such a display again, I'll report you to Gestapo Headquarters at Buckingham Palace without delay," Watson shouted over his shoulder. Then sighed with relief and shame.

***

The street ahead was blocked by two police sedans parked bumper to bumper, as well as razor wire and a gate. My eyes were tearing, not only from the schnapps hangover, but also because the blue-coloured lenses I'd put in were bloody irritating. I took my place in the queue, straightened my tie, and buttoned my coat.

There were four clerical workers ahead of me, going through their daily routine before clocking into their jobs in the government offices that lay beyond. The police man at the gate was a veteran of the force, though the spidery veins in his nose indicated he was given to drink even while on duty. Unfortunately, he didn't appear the least bit intoxicated.

"Papers!" he growled at me, his massive hand snatching my identity papers; which he subjected to, I thought, a more rigorous examination then he did my predecessors.

"Here, what's wrong with your eyes?"

"Summer allergies, sir," I replied, wiping the tears with my handkerchief.

"Where do you work?"

"City Police Headquarters, sir."

"I can read! *Where* do you work?"

"Records Department, sir."

"Never saw you there."

"It's a very big department, sir, as you know. I've gotten myself lost in those sub-basements so many times I'm embarrassed to admit it. So far, no one's noticed. You won't tell anyone, sir, will you?"

He smiled, showing chipped front teeth. "Nah! You're all right, lad! But don't make it a habit, someone's bound to notice sooner rather than later!"

"Thank you, sir!" I pushed on and into the lion's den.

Once ensconced at a desk in a remote corner of one of those sub-basements, I searched through the files dealing with recent police and security forces operations; specifically having to do with the whereabouts of Elliot and his family.

Instead, I came across something that made my blood run cold: yesterday, the City Police rounded up five children – four boys and a girl – and turned them over to the Gestapo for questioning.

***

"You don't think?"

"I don't know, Watson. For many years, the Irregulars and I have perfected a system by which I know they are well. However, I have not heard from Wiggins, and that is long overdue."

"Oh, no," Mrs Hudson cried.

We had met up in Southwark at the abandoned Asylum Chapel in Peckham.

"Try not to worry, Mrs Hudson. None of them will talk, and they're not known to the police, let alone the Gestapo."

"No," Watson remarked. "But they are known to Lestrade."

"Not by sight, or as individuals, Watson. Only as *The Irregulars.*"

Inspector Lohmann came in, carrying two loaves of bread in his hand, two bottles of wine and a wedge of Stilton in the other, a string of sausages hanging from his shoulder. His smile vanished when he saw our concerned expressions.

"What did I miss?"

***

When the lights came on, Wiggins squinted and flinched, the chains of his shackles clattered against the metal chair as he forced them open to look for rats. Ozzie, Rohan, Simpson, and Pilar's eyes were wide as saucers, cheeks tear-streaked, as they did the same.

"Everyone all right?" Wiggins asked quietly, his voice hoarse from screaming.

They all nodded.

"No bites?"

One after the other shook their heads after checking legs and arms.

Keys rattled and the door opened with a shriek. Beckert came in dressed in an impeccably pressed black suit, every hair in place. His protruding eyes slid snail-like over each child. He patted his stomach.

"I've just eaten the most delicious steak supper I think I've ever had!" Then he pulled a handful of hard sweets from his pocket, unwrapped two and popped them into his mouth, and sucked on them loudly. He placed one on the concrete floor in front of each child, as he spoke, "I can't get enough of these! I trust you've been persuaded by the things of the dark to answer all of my questions now."

None of the Irregulars spoke.

"Any who speak will be fed and free to go."

The kids, scared and hungry, fidgeted, but their mouths remained tightly shut.

Beckert ambled over whistling, and pushed all the sweets together into a pile in front of Pilar. "You're Roma, aren't you?"

Pilar blinked and shook her head. "Spanish, sir."

Beckert put his hands on his knees and leaned forward for a closer look. "Spanish? Generalissimo Franco is a close ally of the Reich, did you know that?"

"Yes, sir! He is a great man!"

"Hawthorn, what do you know of phrenology?" Beckert said, measuring Pilar's head from temple to jaw, and the space between her eyes.

"I scored highly on my exams."

"*And?*"

"Oh, Spanish, definitely, Major."

Beckert nodded, then hissed, "*Untermensch*" in Pilar's ear.

"I'll talk," Wiggins interferred.

"Oh?" Beckert replied, eyebrows raised and stood before him. "And what is it you will talk about?"

"Anything you want, Major. I just want to help, have something to eat, and get out of here. Besides, I can be of great help to you and the Reich out on the streets."

"Filthy traitor," Simpson screamed, his face as red as his hair.

"Nazi lover," Rohan shouted.

Hawthorn stormed forward and punched Rohan in the face. "I'll have you deported for that! How do the work camps of the Raj sound to you, coolie?!"

Ozzie and Pilar joined in against Wiggins, the stone walls echoed with the din.

"Quiet!" Beckert bellowed, hands curled into fists so tight his knuckles were white. "Detective Sergeant Hawthorn, *I* will decide *who* is to be deported, and *where*! Is that clear?!"

"Sir!"

"Get out!"

Alone with the children, Beckert gathered up the sweets then methodically laid a trail of them from the rat doors onto their laps. "I have a confession to make. I hate these things, but *the rats* love them!"

"Major," Wiggins said evenly, "I was telling the truth."

"We shall see." Beckert replied and kicked the rat door at his feet. The rodents on the other side squealed shrilly, joined by their fellows across the room. He kicked the doors again and again, laughing and whistling while stirring the rats to a frenzy.

The door swung open. Inspector Lestrade strode through, accompanied by two burly PCs.

"Major Beckert, why are you wasting valuable time on street rats?!"

"I am not wasting time, Inspector. I am doing my duty," Beckert shrieked.

"And how would these kids be involved with a political assassination? You two," Lestrade said to the uniformed police, "remove those restraints and release them."

"Not the girl!"

"Why not?"

Beckert's lower lip trembled. "*She* is important to my investigation."

"You kids can keep the candy," Lestrade shrugged.

"No thanks, sir," Wiggins said, leading the others out. "We don't like 'em."

"Lestrade, you idiot! I believe those vermin are the Baker Street Irregulars!"

"*Them?!* Doubtful, Major. When you've been at this job as long as I have, and know London as I do, you develop a sense about people. It hasn't failed me yet. Good day!"

"Let's go to my office, my dear," Beckert whispered to Pilar. "Where it is much more comfortable."

***

"I couldn't do nothin', Mr Holmes," Wiggins said, tears streaming down his face. "Pilar looked so scared."

"There, there," Mrs Hudson said, her attempt to comfort angrily shrugged off.

"Here son, take a belt of this," Lohmann handed over his flask.

Wiggins took a hard gulp and coughed even harder. His face turned red.

"Well now I'll be able to earn my keep." Lohmann shared a glance with Holmes. "Unless you have a better idea?"

Silence.

"Then I'll be off. Back soon."

"Where is he going?"

"Gestapo Headquarters, Watson," I replied. "To get Pilar."

"Jolly good."

Wiggins sprang up and went after him. "He might need our help!"

***

Lohmann stuck a cigar into the side of his mouth and ignited it with a match. *Now comes the tricky part.*

The gate stood before him, and Buckingham Palace loomed beyond that, its once hallowed facade draped with huge swastika banners that cascaded from roof to trimmed shrubbery. He walked through the gate without challenge, flashing his warrant disc, then entered the foyer dominated by portraits of Hitler in the centre; Himmler, and Goebbels flanking the Grand Staircase. Phones rang constantly, their din along with the voices of those going about their business reminded Lohmann of a beehive about to swarm.

"Can I help you, sir?"

The Inspector found himself confronted by a very young, wide-eyed corporal.

"Direct you. I-I can guide you to whatever department you need."

"That's very good of you, Corporal. Thank you," Lohmann replied, " First, I need you to place a call to Major Beckert's office and ask him to meet me here."

"Of course, sir, and what shall I say is the subject?"

"It has to do with the prisoner in his custody. The Kripo has information on her he requires."

"Right away, sir!" The corporal said, stopped abruptly. "And your name, sir?"

"Inspector Gunther."

The corporal dashed off.

Lohmann puffed his cigar and turned to a matronly woman. "Pardon me. Could you direct me to the offices of the Gestapo?"

"Certainly, up the staircase, then follow the corridor to the right."

"Thank you, madam."

Several men in long trench coats nodded to him as they went past. He came to a suite of offices and took a seat to observe the professional, but harried receptionist. There was a bank of desks, each with a green glass lamp, phone, and blotter occupied by a Gestapo man. Cigarette smoke hung blue in the air.

Then Beckert walked past him. Lohmann wasn't even certain if he was noticed, but thought the man glanced his way. When he was gone, the Inspector waited for a moment, then strode down the corridor to Beckert's office. He walked in, then opened the door to the inner office.

"You must be Pilar. I've heard so much about you. Shall we go?"

Closing the doors behind them, Lohmann put his hand on Pilar's shoulder and they walked past the men busy at their desks and the pretty receptionist busy on the phone. Down the hallway they walked, the Grand Staircase just ahead. Lohmann glanced over the railing and spotted Beckert talking to the corporal, his hands and arms gesticulating wildly.

"Uh oh. Didn't happen to notice a back way out of here, did you, leibchen?"

"No, but I saw a clerk coming up from those back steps over there, bringing the post."

Beckert pointed at the flustered corporal like a pistol and turned to the staircase.

"Lead the way," Lohmann said.

They were down, through the gate, and on their way to Peckham by the time Beckert sounded the alarm.

"Thanks for the thought," Lohmann quipped to Wiggins who stared openmouthed at the pair of them. "But our girl here had everything under control."

"Never had a doubt," Wiggins said, softly punching Pilar's shoulder. Tears of relief threatening to brim over.

***

The pretty receptionist stood up as several men rushed to Beckert's office.

"Search the building," he screamed, eyes popping from their sockets, apoplectic and enraged. "You! Who was in my office?!"

The receptionist's mouth worked, but nothing came out.

"Speak!"

"I didn't notice anyone, Major."

The crowd of Gestapo men that had formed outside looked at each other.

"Don't just stand there! Find them" Beckert shrieked.

Buckingham Palace echoed with alarm klaxons.

**

I waited in the damp shadows of an abandoned warehouse near the Thames. Shadows that moved of their own volition across concrete walls that dripped with condensation as though they already had been consigned to a watery grave.

Fat rats nearly the size of cats roamed about freely, taking no notice of me, at least not right away. One in particular very boldly walked up to me, its nails tapping against the floor. It regarded me with its beady black eyes, whiskers twitching, squeaking loud and high-pitched. I brought my boot down hard, just missing its snout, the sharp sound jarring a flock of feral pigeons from their dark roosts. The big rat held its ground, intimidated not at all.

A shadow grew on the wall the other side of the warehouse. It crawled up the wall like a man was turning into a giant, but the darkness at the ground level concealed his approach, as did his silence; monstrous shoulders that took up the entire wall, a flat hat perched atop a misshapen head. The mutant rat realized his presence too late as a large boot kicked it squeaking into the dust-choked air to splat red and bloody into the wall.

"So, you hate rats too." I said. "Good to know."

The man known as The Creeper smiled, his face coming into a patch of light – a frightening sight to behold. Acromegaly had reshaped his features, giving him a brutish Neandertal-like appearance. He towered over me. He could, without any effort, pick me up, hold me over his head, and snap my back like a dried twig. Glad he's on my side.

"I got your message," he said.

"We start tomorrow."

"About time. As agreed?"

I nodded. "Take them in any order you'd like."

"Ta."

As I watched, The Creeper simply faded into the shadows that clung to everything like a leech. No sound. No movement. He was simply there one moment, gone the next.

***

From across Brick Lane, I watched Elliot's father's tailor shop. I observed no police, Gestapo, or anyone for that matter. Indeed, the establishment was lit, open, and doing a brisk business. How interesting.

I crossed the street to get a closer look. Passerby, street vendors, and all others were as they appeared: denizens of Brick Lane. In the time it takes to turn one's back, I'd applied a trim moustache and round tortoise-framed glasses, and set a black bowler atop my head.

The bell attached to the door rang pleasantly when I stepped in.

Dylan O'Dan, Elliot's father, a strapping thin, tightly muscled man worked needle and thread for a customer as four others whom I recognised as living in this neighbourhood waited. "Elliot! Get out here! Now!"

The rough-sewn burlap curtain parted, and Elliot hurried out. "Yes, Da?"

"Give each of these fine people a number, lad. Be with you in no time at all, folks! No one's turned away in my shop!"

Elliot looked each customer in the eye with a discerning gaze, including myself, handing out a ticket - but he didn't recognise me.

"Off ya go," his father said. "Back to sweeping with ya!"

"Yes, Da!"

The patrons around me exclaimed, "What a good lad he is!" and "So industrious!" among other accolades. His father, Dylan, beamed like the sun when I said, "Just like his da!"

The bell chimed, the door opened, and someone took their place behind me. I turned, tipped my hat and nodded. Inspector Lestrade nodded back. Elliot scampered through the curtain and handed him a ticket.

"Thank you, lad," Lestrade said, chuckling at Elliot disappearing into the back room. "Like a magic act, he is! Look how fast he disappears!"

Dylan O'Dan finished up the first customer, shut the til, and welcomed the next.

Lestrade tapped my shoulder. "What're you here for?"

"Hole in my jacket," I said, and showed him. "Bloody street cars. Hooked it getting off. Why the conductors aren't trained to watch and make certain a body's actually off the bloody thing I'll never understand."

"You could've been killed."

"Too bloody right."

"Me too."

"I beg your pardon?"

"Oh, no, I wasn't almost killed by a streetcar! Me too, meaning I've got a bloody hole, and a missing button on my coat for extras. See?"

I looked and nodded sympathetically, "Too bad."

"Dylan O'Dan there will fix it right as rain in a blink. I always come here."

"I know I will from now on. The business he does here tells the tale."

"It always does," Lestrade said, gently nudging me forward. "Look, you're next in line."

"That was fast!"

"There's no tailor faster in the whole of London!"

The customer in front of me left happy and content. Now it was only O'Dan, Lestrade, Elliot, and myself in the shop when the bell chimed anew the door shut. I heard the bolt being drawn. A great burly PC stood in front of the door. The same PC I encountered at the gate the other day.

"Papers." Lestrade ordered, flashing his police identification.

"Certainly," I replied, taking them out of my coat. "Have I done something wrong?"

"Hmmm. What do you do for a living, Mr Smedley?"

"Doesn't my occupation appear on my documents?"

Lestrade clenched his teeth, his jaw jutting forward. "I can *read*, but I want *you* to *tell* me. Or shall I ask PC Cuff here to teach you some manners?"

PC Cuff displayed his chipped front teeth to me in a very unpleasant smile.

"Oh no! That won't be necessary, sir. I deal, rather, *used* to deal in rare books. Books that have been deemed degenerate by the Reich Home Office. Of late I keep myself employed by giving appraisals."

"I see. And what brings you to the East End?"

"Why, same as you, sir. A client told me of the first-rate work Mr O'Dan does."

"Haven't I seen you somewhere?" Cuff asked, suddenly looking very closely at me. Pock-scarred face bobbing inches from mine.

"What's that, Cuff?" Lestrade asked, still examining my papers.

I waved my hand in front of my nose and squinted my eyes. I could smell the whiskey emanating from his pores. Cuff reared back – he got my hint. I was impressed.

"Well, Cuff, out with it! What did you say?" Lestrade demanded.

Cuff looked at me. I winked at him.

"Nothing, Inspector. My mistake."

"All right, Mr Smedley, you're free to go." Lestrade said, handing back my documents.

"Not until Mr O'Dan mends this bloody hole."

"Get on with it, O'Dan," Lestrade said smiling. "Customer's waiting."

"Right you are, sir." The tailor said. "You're next."

"Tomorrow. Come on, Cuff."

Once alone, I said, "So, what news of the Irish Republican Army?"

"You can count on us, Mr Holmes." Dylan O'Dan whispered.

"Splendid. Tomorrow it begins. Details to follow."

***

The car driven by Cuff with Lestrade in the front left passenger seat made a U-turn, then parked at the kerb.

"Are you absolutely sure, Cuff?" Lestrade asked, passing his flask.

"Sure as I was born, Inspector," Cuff said, taking a large throat-burning slug. "It's him."

"Well, well, well. *Sherlock Holmes.* Things are looking up." He picked up the radio. "All Units. Repeat: All Units, Operation Deerstalker now initiated. You have your orders; follow them to the letter. I expect up to the minute reports in real time. Move!"

"Now Inspector?"

"No! Wait until Holmes leaves and is out of sight. Later."

***

Elliot was nervous, agitated, and could not sleep. The clock just turned three. He got up for a drink of water, and to share his anxiety with his Da when he spotted large shadows standing outside the shop. The window and door shattered inward in a blizzard of glass and splinters, as did the back door.

"Up, up, up! Police!"

Elliot hid in the slim cabinet beneath the display case as heavy boots pounded up the stairs to his family's apartment.

"You fenian bastard!" Elliot heard Lestrade shouting at his Da. "You'll hang for this!"

His mother and sister were crying

"Leave my family out of this, Inspector," his Da said. "They are not part of this. They're innocent!"

"No one's innocent! They'll dance at the end of a rope right next to you! Find the boy! He has to be here!" Lestrade roared.

Then Elliot was alone with the police and the sounds of the shop being torn apart.

***

"*Blimey,*" Wiggins whispered at the destruction done to the tailor shop. *The bastards had done a right bloody job,* he thought, picking through the debris. Wiggins waited for hours until all the bloody British storm troopers left, then ducked under the police tape crisscrossed on the front and back doors and plastered over the windows.

The tape read: *"Entry Forbidden By Order of the Police. Looters Will Be Shot on Sight."*

Upstairs, the O'Dan family apartment was shredded as if wild animals had been let loose with tooth and claw. Wardrobes shattered pieces of wood, bureaus that looked like an axe had been taken to them, every drawer taken out contents upended and piled on the floor. Nothing was spared, not even religious statues.

Wiggins picked his way carefully down the stairs and headed for the back door when he heard a small movement behind him. To his disbelieving eyes, Elliott wriggled his way out of a space so small Wiggins doubted could fit a faery or sprite. He helped the boy stand on his feet, but it was a slow go, as he was so stiff, he could barely move.

"Took your time gettin' here," Elliot said, his face white as a ghost, once he'd gained his legs.

"Had to wait until your guests left, hadn't I?" Wiggins quipped back, smiling.

Elliot grimaced and fell against him.

"Come on, lad. Let's get you somewhere safe."

The two of them disappeared into the twisting cobbled mostly uncharted back lanes of London.

***

Dylan O'Dan sat naked and manacled to a rusted chair under the light of a hanging bare bulb. One eye was swollen

58

tightly shut, the other well on its way. He spit out some teeth. *Well, I can still have my puddings,* he thought blackly optimistic.

The big fella who beat him was good at his job. Very good. He made a very brief, very painful survey and reckoned that only one, maybe two ribs were broken. He pursed his cracked and split lips using the stinging pain to focus on. *Could be worse,* he thought, spitting out more teeth.

The door at the far end of the room opened with a shriek that set his every nerve ending on edge. The big bloke stomped in.

"Hi, love," Dylan O'Dan offered a wide bloody smile. "Missed me so soon?"

***

Wiggins half-supported, half-carried Elliot O'Dan through the tunnel-like labyrinth of the City's back streets and finally came to the turning, well past curfew, that would lead them to the Asylum Chapel Peckham; into the path of young laughing men and women all done up in evening clothes. Shoving the both of them back into the alley from which they'd come, Wiggins hoped they'd not been spotted.

"Don't be scared," a feminine voice called liltingly through the archway. "Come out, we only want to play!"

Two men stood in the archway, backlit, their shadowy heads reaching Elliot and Wiggin's feet.

"Go and get the guttersnipes, girls!" He was talking to a couple of society girls, the fabric of their dresses silvery diaphanous made see-through by the streetlights.

"Don't make a sound, " Wiggins whispered, pushing his and Elliot's back as far against the wall as possible. They'd remain unseen until the girls were right on top of them.

The one with platinum blonde hair giggled as she pulled a straight razor from her gold lamé clutch purse. It positively glittered in the light.

"Oooh, I love to hunt," her companion with bright red hair cooed as she produced a razor of her own.

"Be a lamb and hold these, will you?" The blonde handed their purses to the man.

"Leave some for us," one fellow said.

"Not a chance."

The group laughed, and four shadows watched from the street, laughing, drinking, and egging the two girls on. They stepped in, leaning against each other, giggling as both peered blindly into the shadows ahead, waving their razors with practiced ease.

"Come out, come out, you lovelies."

If not for the lethal blades flashing like lightning, Wiggins might have been tempted to have a go.

"No?" The redhead pouted. She smiled and hissed like a cat while dragging her blade against the brick.

"This keeps 'em nice and sharp-like," the blonde said, doing the same.

"The better to *cut street trash* with."

They were laughing like they were having the time of their lives. Both girls moved ever closer with caution. Elbows bent, hands gripping the slasher's pearl handles with confidence. Each footfall carefully placed, they bounced on the balls of their dainty feet like bare knuckle boxers.

In the time it takes to inhale, we'd be found, Wiggins thought, *and slashed to ribbons.* Sweat dripped down his jaw line. He swallowed dry and coughed.

***

Southwark had never seen such excitement.

The dilapidated Asylum Chapel Peckham was lit up by no less than a dozen City Police cars, their blue lights flashing. Police, Public Order Squad, and Scotland Yard surrounded it.

"You! Inside! Come out with your hands up," Lestrade's voice was amplified to a god-like volume by his megaphone. "Ready to go in, Squad Leader?"

"On your order, Inspector."

"Sherlock Holmes, surrender yourself and your compatriots now, peacefully, or we come in shooting!"

"That traitor will never surrender, Inspector," said the Squad Leader, a British Nazi to his core.

Lestrade glanced at him, taking in the dueling scar and toothbrush moustache. "No, Squad Leader Chetcher, I don't believe he will either. You may proceed."

The martinet grinned, adjusting his thick spectacles. "All right, men, tear gas canisters loaded?"

"Yes, sir," his aide replied.

"Gas masks on, service sidearms loaded and ready."

His aide nodded after checking the men.

"Fire tear gas!"

The air was sliced by the sounds *thump, thump, thump*. The canisters all hit their targets, mainly the entrance doorway and windows.

"In, in, in!" Chetcher shouted, voice muffled by his gas mask, as he led his black uniformed men into the derelict building. Twenty minutes later, they came back out.

"Well?"

"Place is empty, Inspector Lestrade. It's been empty for a very, very long time by the looks of things."

"That's impossible! Sherlock Holmes was seen going in there not thirty minutes ago!"

Chetcher shook his head. "Well, he isn't now. The gas is cleared, in case you'd like to have a look for yourself."

"You and your men may return to barracks, Squad Leader."

"Yes, sir. Thank you, sir."

Lestrade slammed the megaphone down on the hood of his car. "Bryan, Daniels, let's go."

"I just don't figure it, Inspector," DS Bryan said, the light from his torch illuminating a turned over table in the corner, several dust-covered chairs arranged in the middle of the room for a service that would never be held. "The tip came from a verified source."

"Daniels, take the car and PC Cuff, and bring that *reliable* source in for questioning."

"Sir."

"And Daniels."

"Yes, sir?"

"Have Cuff soften him up, so he's ready to talk when I get back."

"Sir."

"Bryan, secure another vehicle. I'm going to be a bit longer."

Lestrade walked every inch of the floor and found *nothing*. No indication of habitation, except rodents and birds. He smiled in spite of this, feeling in his gut that he was getting closer.

***

As if joined, the two girl's heads snapped like predators, and smiled. "You see, Pru, I *knew* they'd get bored."

"Cough again, won't you love? Still too dark to see."

A huge shape, blacker than the shadowy gloom, put itself between Wiggins, Elliot, and the girls. Large hands grabbed hold of the girls' heads, lifted their long legs kicking in the air, and slammed them together with a sickening thud; their razors fell tinkling to the cobbles.

"Hey!" The pack of men and women waded into the narrow lane, waving truncheons and razors. In the confined space they fared even poorer than the girls who lay at Wiggins and Elliot's feet, choking on their own blood.

Wiggins covered the younger boy's eyes, but both heard bones being shattered, skulls broken against the brick and cobbles, and the screams.

The giant turned to them, an otherworldly silence descended like a sheet to conceal the carnage around them, and tipped his flat hat. "You boys all right?"

"I-It's The Creeper! Wiggins," Elliot exclaimed, eyes wide. "*The Creeper!*"

Wiggins couldn't take his eyes off the man's face.

"Saw you were in a spot of trouble and came to help out. Now get on, the police will be on this before you know it," the hideous man said gently.

"Thank you," Wiggins nodded. The Creeper was human after all. "Come on, Elliot. Thanks ag…" When he turned around, the giant had vanished, leaving only a trail of bodies behind. "We're going to have to take the long way round, lad."

***

"Beckert here," the Gestapo operative said into the phone.

"Major, the body of another Metropolitan Policeman has been discovered," Detective Sergeant Hawthorn spoke from the other end.

"Bring my car."

The corpse lay sprawled across the paws of one of the lions in Trafalgar Square; its slit throat gaped red and opened like a second mouth.

"Look at that, displayed for all to see," Hawthorn sneered. "Like a side of beef at the butcher's."

"Same as the first, Dr Michaels?"

"Without doubt, Major Beckert. As distinctive as a fingerprint."

Beckert examined the body closely. "PC 347 Geoffrey Baker. Do you know him, Hawthorn?"

"Never saw him before now, Major."

"Dr Michaels?"

"No, Major," the obese coroner replied, his pink jowls wiggling with each shake of his head.

"Detective Sergeant Hawthorn, redouble your efforts and interview your fellow officers. This case must be closed!"

***

The entire tenement reeked with the odour of death.

"How long has he been dead?" Lestrade held his handkerchief to his nose.

"Two, three weeks I'd say, Inspector," Daniels replied.

Lestrade looked upon the blackened bloated face, and the blue-bottle flies tucking in. "This would have been the sort of end I'd predicted for old Jock here."

"Looks like someone folded him in half, broke his back."

"Remind you of anyone?"

"Course. The Creeper."

Lestrade nodded.

"He hasn't been heard from for a long time. What beef do you suppose he had with Jock?"

"Don't know."

"Suppose he knew Jock was one of our informants?"

"Not only ours, Daniels, our man here was also on friendly terms with our pals in the Gestapo."

"Wait a moment, didn't the Gestapo raid this place?"

"Yes! I remember hearing about it. Two, three weeks ago."

"Get me the recording of the call Jock made, Daniels."

"Sir."

Daniels had the requested tape cued up for Lestrade back at the Yard. All tips and denunciations are recorded, regardless of whether they were placed with the Gestapo or the Yard.

"I want to report that a German has taken a room at my place. He's hiding from something, I'm sure of it. The name he give me was Gunther," Jock said.

***

"We found nothing, Inspector Lestrade. The place was unfit for rats, let alone a citizen of the Reich," an SS man said over the phone.

"But the informant's been very reliable in the past."

"That may be, sir, but…. Wait a moment, the place actually smelled good to me."

"I beg your pardon?"

"It smelled like the cigars my grandfather smoked."

"Cigars? Do you know any Germans named Gunther?"

The SS man laughed. "Of course! Besides myself, there are thousands of us! If there's nothing else I can do for you, sir, I really am quite busy."

"One more thing. Why would the tenement have been raided by the Gestapo on the strength of our informant's tip?"

"Afraid I can't tell you, Inspector, the matter has been classified. Gestapo access only."

"Many thanks," Lestrade said and rang off.

"No luck, sir?" Daniels asked from the doorway.

"A Gestapo-contrived dead-end. Something's up though." Lestrade pressed a button and spoke, "Evie, be a dear and get Major Beckert on the phone."

"Yes, Inspector."

Daniels looked skeptical.

"I know, but I have to find out what's going on with this mysterious German named Gunther who takes the worst room in the East End, and why a tip from a British slumlord prompts a raid by the Gestapo."

"Time to offer the hand of British-German Friendship," Daniels said. "I'll boil some hot water to wash our hands afterwards."

Lestrade smiled wryly and waited for the phone to ring.

**

PC 179 Archie Croft blew his whistle until he ran out of air. Then he vomited, fortunately spewing the street rather than all those broken bloody bodies strewn about the dark narrow lane.

Lestrade was called to the scene twenty minutes later.

"What a mess," Dr Michaels said, pushing his rimless spectacles up his bulbous nose, his fingers red with blood. He sighed and grunted from the exertion.

"Any ideas?"

"At first glance, I'd say they were set upon by a gang wielding mallets and hammers, given the frightful abundance of blunt force trauma that's been inflicted."

"But?"

"Upon further examination I'd say a person, or persons, killed our young friends with their bare hands."

Lestrade stooped down and pointed out several cut-throat razors and truncheons that littered the cobbles lying in and out of puddles of blood and brain matter.

Michaels shrugged. "I'm not implying it wasn't deserved, Inspector. All London avoids them."

"Any signs whoever did this was injured in the melee?"

"Unknown. My men are sweeping the lane for evidence, as well as Scotland Yard. However, you'll need to go around so as not to disturb the scene."

"Thank you. I am well aware of proper police procedure, Dr Michaels."

"Of course! It's just I'm so beastly hot at the moment. My apologies, Inspector."

"Inform me if and when any of the dead are identified."

"That may be difficult, given the damage done to the faces, Inspector Lestrade, but several purses and other odds and ends have already been recovered and bagged."

"Carry on."

"Inspector?"

"Yes?"

"Another PC was found in Trafalgar Square, his body lying across the paws of one of the lions."

"Throat cut?"

"Yes, sir. By the same hand as well."

"Do you think the two are political?"

"It's possible; anything is in this day and age."

"Indeed." Lestrade walked to his car, thinking he should be hearing from his man inside Gestapo Headquarters soon.

"He's primed and ready downstairs, sir." Bryan informed Lestrade when he returned to the Yard.

"So, Terry, I'm certain that PC Cuff here has informed you why you've been brought in."

"Nobody's said nothin'! Look what he did to my face!"

"Funny thing happened when we acted on your tip, Terry," Lestrade said, turning a chair backwards and taking a seat. "Sherlock Holmes wasn't there, no one was."

"I saw him, as God is my witness I did!"

"You embarrassed me, Terry. Imagine how I felt sending in the Public Order Squad, tear gas, the whole shebang! And all I found was rat and bird shite." Lestrade put his mouth near the prisoner's bleeding ear. "Stepped in some too."

"I ain't lyin' to ya, Inspector!"

"Cuff!"

"No, please!"

"Take him to a cell, the darkest one you can find. Taking you out of circulation, Terry. Who knows, a week – or six months – in the dark might bring out an honest streak in you."

As Terry was dragged away, Lestrade frowned.

He didn't have that kind of time.

***

I wanted to smash my head into the wall. I'd underestimated Lestrade. *Lestrade!*

Not only did it nearly cost all our lives; my entire plan of revenge would have collapsed. England would have been

72

entrenched in tyranny for decades to come, ultimately tearing itself apart in a national orgiastic suicide that would eclipse the Fall of Rome.

I would make all of Nazi England pay for my mistake in blood.

***

Professor Moriarty sat in the dark, thinking. Every fibre of his being focused on Dr Mabuse and his demise – a foregone conclusion; but *how* swift, or slow, and bloody was what the Napoleon of Crime was currently occupied by.

And reveling in.

After all, *he,* Professor James Moriarty, rules the criminal underworld alone. Now and forever.

He smiled broadly.

The decision had been made.

And set in motion.

***

Hans Beckert was never an investigator. Yet he'd taken over the inquiry into the murders of policemen; *English* bobbies! What did he care for dead bobbies? At the time it seemed a good idea, what with that officious Inspector Lestrade lording over the scene, the centre of attention.

What were you thinking, he asked himself over and over. And despaired.

The office fell suddenly silent.

Beckert's mouth went dry and his blood turned to ice when *Der Nachtwandler* entered his office. Dr Mabuse's reanimated corpse, its features frozen and waxy, turned and silently regarded him after closing the door. It was as though the Earth herself held her breath.

Two pinpricks of light grew in the centre of The Sleepwalker's black-as-night glasses. The lipless mouth parted slightly with the unmistakable voice of Dr Mabuse. "Beckert, you are to turn the investigation into the murdered policemen back over to Scotland Yard."

"Sir, I am quite capable of—"

"No! It is obvious to me that you are out of your depth. Turn the investigation over to Scotland Yard and Inspector Lestrade immediately!"

"At once, Herr Dr Mabuse."

"Return to your command of the Special Search Book Kommando. Do not fail me."

"I am yours to command, SD Commander," Beckert saluted.

"*I know.*"

As silent as a wraith, the Mabuse automaton left Beckert alone and shaking. Once more sound returned to the world. Typewriters, murmured voices, telephones.

***

Der Nachtwandler backed into his resting place – an unadorned coffin in the darkest corner of Dr Mabuse's vast office taking up the entire top floor of Buckingham Palace.

"Well done, Cesare. Sleep now," Mabuse said, drawing the lid closed. He sat behind his massive desk, took a breath, focused his incredible mind and saw through the eyes of Georg, Spoerri, Pesch, and countless others throughout London. Over the past decades, he'd honed this remarkable ability to a razor-sharp edge.

To build an Empire of Crime, one must *control everyone*.

Through chaos, fear, and horror.

I stand at the precipice of that Empire's realization, he thought *I have eyes everywhere. I see everything. Everyone. You too, Professor Moriarty.*

***

Colonel Sebastian Moran held the Lee Enfield No. 4 sniper rifle easily, making minute adjustments to the 3.5X telescopic sight. In the crosshairs, the centre of the box, where the pasty-faced freak put himself.

But first, Mabuse.

You won't feel a thing, which is a pity, Moran thought, placing his index finger on the trigger he caressed it.

Moriarty sat motionless in the centre of his dark library. He consulted his watch at the precise moment; his synchronization with Moran was perfect— No, *exquisite.*

***

Georg, manservant to Dr Mabuse exited the private elevator and found his master 's lifeless eyes staring back at him, a neat hole bored into the centre of his high forehead.

Cesare, The Sleepwalker was also dead; two bullets had pierced the coffin and his head.

Per previous orders, Georg called Pesch and Spoerri. The Second Phase began, exactly as Dr Mabuse had foreseen.

***

"That was easy," Daniels said. "And painless."

"He said the files will be sent down at once," Lestrade said.

"Think he's up to something?"

The Inspector shook his head, then mouthed the name *Mabuse.*

Daniels nodded.

There was a knock at the door.

"Files from Major Beckert, Inspector Lestrade," reported a young clerk.

"Put them on my desk, if you please, Woodhouse."

"Very good, sir."

The box of files were split between the two men.

"We'll have to start from scratch," Lestrade said, disgusted, but not surprised, shutting the last case folder.

"Bryan and I will start straight away," Daniels added, took the box, and left.

Meanwhile, Lestrade sat back and lit a cigarillo. *Scotland Yard will show them how *real* police work is done.*

***

Hans Beckert was content. *Now* work that he *was* competent at could commence. He missed the little Roma girl; he'd such plans for her, but was confident he'd have her in his hands once again, along with *Herr Gunther,* the Kripo inspector. The Special Search Book Kommando he oversaw was tasked with hunting down and arresting *all* traitors to the Reich. They'd begun with the arrest and execution of Winston Churchill. The coward George and his family, including his daughter Elizabeth fled to Canada. No matter, Beckert thought, Gestapo operatives were keeping them under surveillance – soon they'd be returned to face the hangman.

His priority now was, of course, *Sherlock Holmes*. He lit an Ariston and acquainted himself with the traitor's file.

Afterwards he started another file on someone he long suspected: Inspector Lestrade.

***

The office of Dr Mabuse was securely locked, after Spoerri, Georg, Pesch, and Hawach tidied up. Voice recordings made previously by Mabuse for nearly any and every eventuality were cued up and ready to play at a moment's notice to maintain the illusion that he lived.

Their Phase Two assignments were as follows: Hawach would shadow Beckert, Pesch Mycroft Holmes, while Spoerri kept Lestrade and the Yard under surveillance, and Georg would not only track down Sherlock Holmes, but also the German named Gunther, who Dr Mabuse believed was none other than Kommisar Karl Lohmann, and kill them both.

The two women of the Mabuse gang, Fine and Cara Carozza, the Folies Bergere dancer who loved him, would see to the death of Professor Moriarty.

***

Watson and Mrs Hudson, as well as Inspector Lohmann nodded their understanding of the assignments I'd given them. Professor Moriarty and Colonel Moran looked as though they'd rather be anywhere else.

"Do you understand?" I repeated.

"Of course, dear boy," Moriarty replied in that condescending headmaster's tone.

The whole time, Moran and he grinned like schoolboys harbouring a deep dark secret. What they did in their personal time was their own business, I thought and went on with the briefing.

The only things those two needed to know were because they happened to overlap with Watson, Mrs Hudson, and Lohmann's assignments; the rest I kept to myself.

"Get some rest. The days ahead will offer none."

***

Twenty-four hours had passed. As Mycroft couldn't fail to notice that he still had his head, he ordered Lestrade to continue his search. He nodded with approval while reading the reports on the raid at the Asylum Chapel Peckham in Southwark.

Almost nabbed you there, didn't they, Sherlock, The Minister of the Realm thought. Sherlock had always been naive when it came to politics and statecraft; while Mycroft had always been an Empire man. He saw to it that the rapprochement with Hitler was signed, because it brought peace, stability, and most of all, order to the British Empire. For Mycroft, the Reich-British Alliance was essential to preserve the English way of life. For Sherlock, it was Treason.

Misguided fool, Mycroft thought, lighting a cigar, and ringing for a brandy. *You will die, forever known as a Traitor to the Empire: unmourned, reviled by everyone, and most unforgivable of all, a stain on my legacy. My Judas.*

***

I would discover the secret held by Moriarty and Moran in due time, but now was occupied by more pressing matters – namely the utter decapitation of the traitorous British State, beginning with Mycroft.

The sun may never set on the British Empire, but I observed it rarely cast its light or warmth upon *Fascist England.*

I set out beneath low dark clouds that scuttled like roaches from sudden light from the Waterloo Necropolis Station to The Diogenes Club, and Mycroft. Standing before the once genteel, once grand building, I saw where those dark clouds crawled to; they seemed to roil and congeal like ink directly above it. As darkness fell, the facade was lit by searchlights mounted atop the building, two beams never leaving the entrance, illuminating it as though midday, while four others swept the grounds, moving ghost-like over the barbed wire barriers, and perimeter guard houses situated at the four corners. Papers ready, I made for the servant's entrance round back, precisely on time for the evening staff's arrival. Moments later I was inside.

***

Karl Lohmann watched Hans Beckert enter his house, an extravagant Edwardian terraced townhouse overlooking the Thames. He screwed the silencer to the muzzle of his pistol and entered through the back French doors into the library. He sat in a luxurious leather armchair, helping himself to a whiskey from the Waterford crystal decanter. Pictures of the family the house was stolen from still hung on the mahogany paneled walls, in silver and gold frames on the mantle. Lohmann doubted they were smiling now; or alive.

"No! Nothing," Beckert shouted, just outside the door. "Go home!"

The door swung open and Lohmann leveled his gun. "Don't make any sudden moves, Beckert."

The man froze in his tracks.

"Close and lock the door." Once the Major had complied, Lohmann continued, "Turn around slowly, put your hands up, my gun is aimed at your black heart."

"You'll never leave here alive," Beckert hissed.

"Neither will you."

"*You,*" Beckert gasped, eyes wide.

"Call me *Gunther,*" Lohmann said. "Been a long time, *M.* You've gone down in the world. Way down."

"I've come up, flat foot. The Nazis gave me purpose, honed and sharpened me into the dagger of a man I am today. Those five long years ago in Berlin, I was weak, pathetic, driven by the monster inside. The Nazis taught me to focus *him, his* urges."

"I saved you from that kangaroo court that was moments away from hanging your sorry behind."

"Wrong again, fat man. The Nazis saved me."

Lohmann's pistol coughed at the same time Beckert fired his. Beckert smiled and moved forward a step before noticing the hole in the centre of his chest. Blood poured from his mouth and he crumpled noiselessly to the floor. A pathetic puppet whose strings had been cut. Lohmann made sure there was no pulse, then he finished the whiskey and left the way he came. As he walked along the Victoria Embankment, he noticed he was bleeding.

***

Hawach had settled in to watch Beckert's place, taking a couple generous swigs of schnapps from his flask, the car's warm interior and comfortable seat lulling him to a doze when he thought he heard a pistol shot. He straightened and looked around. The sound came again, but this time it was from a car parked up the block; its frustrated owner kicked the door savagely.

Ah, Hawach thought, *that's what it was.* He tipped his flask at the hapless motorist, took another swig, and closed his eyes. Surveillance did not suit him; soon he fell asleep. In his dream he stood on an empty street, a tall man stood in front of him.

What am I doing in this line, Hawach asked the man's back.

The tall man's head turned three hundred and sixty degrees around, his features obscured in shadow.

That's all right, Hawach stammered suddenly, frightened, *I'll wait.*

Two yellow eyes opened; they glowed like lanterns.

Hawach screamed.

***

"Sir! We have a problem!" DS Daniels said, skidding to a stop outside Lestrade's office.

PC Cuff stared at the bare light bulb that hung from its cord in Interrogation Room Seven, his neck and back broken. Two other guards had their throats cut.

Dylan O'Dan was gone.

"Who unlocked his shackles?" Lestrade asked, examining the bracelets hanging from the chair.

"It had to be one of these two men, Inspector. Cuff would spit in their faces."

"And no one noticed O'Dan leaving the building?"

"The Desk Sergeant told me he saw the prisoner being escorted by two PC's who presented proper Prisoner Transport Papers, Inspector."

"Those Fenian bastards," Lestrade seethed. "Round up all known Irish Republican Army sympathisers and suspects, and put out an escaped prisoner alert. They couldn't have gotten far."

"Already done, sir."

"And issue a murder warrant for The Creeper. Shoot on sight."

"Sir."

84

***

The glowing yellow eyes cast Hawach in their evil light. "Wake Up! Fool!"

Mabuse's henchman jolted awake, the voice of his master still echoing in his ears. Hawach tossed his flask out the car window and sat up straight. The front door was locked, so he walked around Beckert's house looking for an easy way in. Around back, he saw the French doors that opened onto the patio were open. He noticed blood drops on the flagstones. They led away from the doors, a few drops beaded on the lawn, then disappeared. Hawach pulled his gun, and went in. He flicked his torch on as it was too dark. The beam fell on the body of Major Hans Beckert, who was indeed very, very dead.

Finding the light switch, Hawach turned them on, found a phone, and rang Georg.

"You didn't touch anything, did you?"

"What do you take me for?"

"Did you?"

"Of course not."

"Right, leave now and report to Cara. I'll take care of it."

"All right, Georg."

The faces of Dr Watson, Mrs Hudson, and Colonel Moran glowed white clustered around a lantern and four packs of plastic explosives. They were in a sub-basement of Buckingham Palace. Their job? To attach the explosive charges to each load bearing pillar around them.

"Where's Inspector Lohmann?" Watson spoke.

"I haven't seen him, I hope he's all right," Mrs Hudson replied.

"We can't wait around for him," said Moran. "Set them, then run like Hell."

"For how long?"

The Colonel sighed heavily. "Five minutes, Mrs Hudson, as explained to you."

"Don't take a tone with me, you foul man."

Moriarty's majordomo chuckled. "Madam, you don't know the half of it."

"It doesn't look like enough to me," Watson said, fixing his charge to the pillar.

"When all of these blow, Dr Watson, the Palace and SD Headquarters will fall like a house of cards. Believe me, these will do."

"Set," Mrs Hudson said.

"Set," Watson said.

"Right, flip your switch on three. One, two, three,"
Moran instructed. "Now go!"

***

Cara Carozza, Fine, and Hawach stood across the
street from the building Moriarty was in. They'd been joined
by the two most vicious packs of Bright Young Things that
Nazi England had ever produced – both responsible for the
murders of the homeless and destitute. Their leaders – a pale
young man wearing a monocle, with gleaming black hair
ending in ringlets sporting a pointed Van Dyke, and an even
younger woman perhaps nineteen, also very pale, with a
severe bob of short straight black hair – stood close together
constantly whispering.

"So, that is where the great Professor Moriarty lives,"
the white-faced man said, smiling. Hawach couldn't help but
notice his teeth had been filed to needle-sharp points.

"*Oh Jack, I can hardly control myself,*" the girl purred,
her ruby-red tongue dancing over her filed teeth.

They kissed loudly and obnoxiously. Both wore
identical signet rings on their left index fingers, gleaming in
the streetlamp's light.

"*All right,* you too," Cara said, exasperated. "You can carry on *after the job.*"

"What do you take me for?!" Jack said, offended. "She's my *sister!*"

"Let's go." Fine rolled her eyes. "You all know what to do."

The brother-sister pack, numbering twenty strong, went right up to the front door of the dark Victorian manse that spanned nearly an entire city block. Cara accompanied them, smoking her ever present Turkish cigarette in its long ivory holder. Fine went around back with the second pack, led by a brutish-looking fellow with one brow, sunken eyes, and hair cut in the fashion of a bowl.

Hawach took over Fine's customary role of lookout.

"What a dump," the sister whined as she looked through a filthy window.

"Moriarty's an old geezer, sis, what did you expect?"

"Quiet," Cara hissed. "Everyone be alert! The Professor is no fool, and there's certain to be guards inside. Guards who'll know the place blindfolded."

"That's what makes this so much fun, silly," said the heiress with sharpened white teeth. "Jack, don't you have that lock picked yet?"

A loud click brought a horrible smile to the girl's face.

"You were saying?" Jack asked as he pushed the doors open. The pack entered unopposed, their movement stirring up dust that hadn't been disturbed in decades.

The girl coughed and sneezed dramatically. "How horrible!"

"Yeah, the so-called *Napoleon of Crime* has really let this place go," Jack laughed.

"And what is that awful smell?"

"Mould, sis. Rot, and a lot of mould."

"Ew, this place is so fuzzy! Look, it's on the walls, and on the sheets covering the furniture!"

"Quiet! I told you, be alert," Cara said. She stopped abruptly, her eyes widened in confusion, and turned around. In the centre of her back was the hilt of a knife buried deep. The woman gasped, her mouth working to form words, but only blood came out, and she fell backwards onto the blade, shuddered, then was still.

"Find where that came from," Jack shouted. "Spread out! Jill with me!"

He and his sister ducked low and crept as close to the wall as they could. Suddenly the sheets around them rose like wraiths. Within minutes, half their number had been cut down. Then eight of the pack were skewered by crossbow bolts that whistled through the foetid dust-filled air. Jack and Jill threw down their razors and blackjacks, and held their hands up high, while blood curdling screams and sounds of battle issued from the rear of the house.

"What do ya think they're going to do to us, Jack?" Jill asked as six white-sheeted splashed with red figures holding dripping swords and daggers closed on them.

***

Hawach wasn't any better at being a lookout than he was at surveillance. Clearly the sound emanating from the great house told him everything he needed to know: Cara and Fine were dying right along with the bloodthirsty aristocrats.

Time to go, he thought, and leaned forward to push the ignition button when he felt a tremendous punch to his neck. Surprise lit his face when he felt the shaft of an arrow. He struggled to draw breath, but Death clutched him in his skeletal hands and took him away.

***

While evading police patrols, Inspector Karl Lohmann took a moment in a filthy corner of a filthy alley to ascertain the extent of his injury. He'd been shot, but fortunately the bullet grazed a path in the fat of his side. It burned like Hell, but he staunched the blood with his handkerchief, confident that he'd live, and headed for his rendezvous with Mabuse.

The plan had been for him to assist Dr Watson, Mrs Hudson, and Moran, however, his exchange with Beckert had likely been a delay they could ill afford to extend. So, he continued on assuming they'd planted the explosives which would give him very little time. He picked up his pace, hissing from the pain flashing from his side with every step.

Buckingham Palace was lit as though it was the King's Jubilee. Lohmann stopped to admire the impressive view, and mostly to catch his breath.

Four low register thuds rippled across the ground and shook his innards. The lights of the Palace flickered then went out. The building leaned left, then right, and began collapsing in on itself. Screams issued from within as windows shattered, then each floor fell, pancaked on top of the other.

The top floor containing the office of Dr Mabuse crashed down, joining the others in the basement and sub-basement; this was followed by several fiery explosions that blew out any windows that somehow remained intact.

Lohmann dove to the pavement, covering his head as the street around him was peppered with bricks, plaster, and glass. When he looked up, all that remained was a ruin of fire, rubble, and the odour of burning flesh. He got on his feet, took out a cigar and lit it, drawing deeply.

Now Mabuse is the Devil's problem, he thought smiling, happily puffing and walking away as a crowd of onlookers formed, and sirens of the police and the fire brigade wailed in the distance.

***

Mycroft blinked at the lamp as it flickered. He went back to the report in front of him when the sound of a massive explosion rolled over the street like thunder, rattling the windows of the Diogenes.

Then the lights went out altogether.

In the darkness, he heard Stevens shout from the outer office, the report of a shot, then something striking the wall followed by a loud sickening crack. When the generator kicked in and the lights came back on he saw me in front of him, along with The Creeper.

"Sherlock."

"Mycroft."

"I see your taste in friends remains consistent."

"At least I have friends."

"That explosion."

"Buckingham Palace."

"You're mad. What you've done will change nothing."

"That remains to be seen."

"What now? Are you going to kill me? Or your friend here perhaps?"

"Oh, it will be me – I don't believe even *he* could lift you."

"There's the small matter of my guards."

"They're all dead. You're alone, Mycroft." I pulled out my Webley and pointed it at him.

The lights went out.

I fired, emptying the chamber.

When they came back on, Mycroft was gone.

"Hands up, *traitors,* " a voice snarled behind us. "Drop the gun and *don't move.* Mustn't cheat the hangman."

I dropped my Webley. Several MP-40 German submachine guns were drawn.

"Both of you, turn around slowly. "

We turned around and stared into the black barrels of the guns, held in the hands of black uniformed SS veteran guards who backed away from us to increase the distance and nullify any idea we had of trying something.

"Now *move!* "

We were led out onto the street where more guards were waiting next to police vans.

"First, Scotland Yard and Inspector Lestrade want a word with you, followed by Special Branch. Then it's *our* turn." The SS commander smiled unpleasantly.

The Creeper and I exchanged a glance before we were prodded and pistol-whipped into separate wagons.

That could've gone better, I thought as the door slammed shut.

As the van took off, I wished for a large whiskey. Or perhaps *two.*

I contented myself with a pipe filled to the brim with the coarsest, harshest shag tobacco on the market. Soon I couldn't see my hand in front of my face due to the thick smoke it produced. It was an added bonus that it stunk to high Heaven.

The driver was coughing his lungs out. "Oy, put that *stinking* rubbish out!"

I ignored him and puffed even faster.

The small metal door slid open.

"Put that out," the driver's mate shouted.

I smiled, but doubted he could even see me. *I* couldn't see *him.*

"Why didn't you cuff him," the driver yelled.

"Why didn't *you*?!"

"Lestrade's gonna have our guts for garters," the driver said. The van lurched left and shuddered to a halt. "Come on! Move it!"

"What's wrong," the voice of the other van's driver called.

"You'd better cuff your prisoner!"

"*You* didn't? *Ours is so much bigger!*"

I heard keys jingling, then inserted into the lock.

"If you say anything to Lestrade, or anyone else, Renfro, you'll pay! I swear!"

"Oh, please don't tell your mum," Renfro mocked. "She's twice the man you are!"

"Bloody bastard," my driver mumbled as he threw open the door. "Stuff it, Renfro!"

"Where the bloody hell is he?!" The two squinted through the smoke that hung around me, stubborn defiantly refusing to dissipate.

"I'll call yer mum right now," Renfro chided, laughing. "*She'll* not hesitate! Oh no, she won't!"

My driver growled, then I heard the roar of engines, the squeal of tyres.

"What the hell" Renfro yelled.

The entire world erupted into shotgun blasts and pistol shots.

"Right, we don't have all day," called a voice with the sweetest Irish brogue I've ever heard.

I emerged from the strangely inert pipe smoke and jumped to the street greeted by four bodies shredded by shells and bullet holes. Four men held guns, their faces covered by masks. Another man freed The Creeper using a bolt cutter.

Shocked passersby started yelling for police, a few even produced whistles.

"*Let's go, lads,*" the leader yelled.

We jumped into the cars and sped away while the IRA men fired over the heads of the bystanders, who scattered like geese.

***

Jack and Jill were pushed and prodded through hallways that seemed endless, sword or dagger tips always at their back.

"Ouch," Jill said, repeatedly.

"Go easy, lads," Jack said. "I say, we're moving, aren't we?"

Their ghostly escorts continued, silent as the tomb, their blades drawing blood.

"Ouch," Jill said again.

"Maybe they're foreigners."

"Bloody foreigners. They should learn the King's English, otherwise they're not welcome in this country."

"Too bloody right."

"Jack, I'm so very tired, where do you think they're taking us?"

"To meet Professor Moriarty, of course. Doubtless he knows all about us, and wants us to work for him."

"*Work?!* How dreadful! We haven't worked a day in our lives. I just want to go home!"

They were ushered into a huge cellar where three massive furnaces squatted like black spiders. In front of them were the bodies of their cohorts, with more being dragged, heads thumping against the stone floor, and added to the growing pile. Their ghostly guard pointed its sword at the pierced bloody corpses, then to the blazing hot opened furnace.

"I want to go home now, Jack."

At sword point, Jack and Jill lifted, carried, and threw the ghastly mutilated bodies of Cara, Fine, Hawach, and their murderous pack-mates into the flames.

"If this is the kind of work Moriarty wants us for, he can bloody well do it himself," Jill shouted, wiping her bloody hands on her cocktail dress.

The pair were each stabbed in the leg. They fell screaming in a heap onto the blood and offal covered stone floor. Then they were thrown alive into the flames. Their screams echoed through the great dark house. And brought a contented smile to Professor Moriarty's lips.

***

Scotland Yard was a hive of activity as reports from still-smouldering Buckingham Palace, as well as the capture and escape of Sherlock Holmes. Inspector Lestrade, Daniels, and Bryan barely kept up with the phone calls and updates from the scenes. So far they'd confirmed the deaths of Major Hans Beckert at his home earlier, and hundreds of dead in the explosion at Buckingham Palace; including Dr Mabuse, the SD Commander-GB himself. nearly the entire contingent of the London Gestapo had been decimated – the number of fatalities was expected to go up when body retrieval became possible. As of now, the explosion site was still burning. And would continue to do so perhaps for days, according to London's fire chief.

The phone rang.

"Lestrade here. Where? Right, on my way."

"Sir?" Bryan inquired.

"There's been another murder of a constable, just down the street."

"Shall I go, sir?"

"No, I'll attend to it. Every man is needed here."

"Inspector," Dr Michaels said. "This has to be the most brazen yet."

Indeed it was. The corpse was on its feet, leaning against a call box. Bled white to the colour of freshly fallen snow, the unfortunate PC wore an expression of utter astonishment. His blood saturated the entire front of his uniform, just beginning to dry to a brown crust.

"Who reported this?" Lestrade .

"That lady over there, sir." The PC first on the scene pointed, then looked frantically about. "She was just there, Inspector! I talked to her myself!"

"What did she look like, Haskins?"

"Very attractive, sir," he replied, blushing. "I thought she must be a film star."

"Her papers?"

"All up to date and in perfect order, Inspector."

"Did you see this woman, Dr Michaels?"

"Alas no, Inspector Lestrade. I was otherwise engaged."

"Quite. All right, Haskins go over there and search your memory and no doubt keen observational skills and try to retrieve her name, address, anything."

"Yes Inspector." Haskins walked off like a man to the gallows.

"PC 831, Clive Street," Dr Michaels read the man's identity card.

"Right, I'll go back to the Yard with Haskins and comb through our records. Perhaps there's something that all our murdered men have in common."

"Until next time, Inspector," the coroner said sardonically.

***

Georg narrowly escaped the explosion and trailed after Lohmann, who he spotted as he waddled down the street puffing like a steam locomotive on his cigar. Dr Mabuse's manservant and assassin smiled, slipping on his killing gloves. He was an ardent believer in synchronicity – and this

100

was just one more instance that affirmed that belief. Quickly he gained on the fat detective who was still brushing dust and ash off his coat and out of his hair. Instead of using Lohmann to locate Sherlock Holmes and the others, Georg decided to kill him now, and save that hunt for another time. The Kripo detective had been a particularly irritating thorn in all their sides for far too long.

As he closed on Lohmann, he slipped out his switchblade, opening it with a click and flash of silver. Time to settle accounts.

Lohmann stopped unexpectedly, forcing Georg to do the same. Then the fat man looked around surreptitiously, took out his flask, and drank deep, his head tipping back.

Wasting no time, Georg moved forward and sunk his blade into Lohmann's heart like a striking viper. He removed it just as swiftly and walked off, not looking back until he'd passed two storefronts.

Lohmann put his flask back in his coat pocket, walked a few steps, then fell face first to the sidewalk. Concerned passersby gathered around him. Georg smiled and lit a cigarette which he puffed from a black onyx holder. The man had not felt a thing – the ledger balanced at last.

***

Mycroft was furious as he slammed the phone on the receiver. Sherlock had escaped *again*. And with him, the monstrous throwback known as The Creeper. The Diogenes had been so securely locked down a fly couldn't gain access.

The elder Holmes issued a death warrant and a shoot-on-sight order for both of them, as well as Mrs Hudson, Dr Watson, and the Irregulars. It was too late for a show trial.

So be it, brother. All out war you shall have.

***

Irene Adler smiled beneath the veil she'd lowered, observing Lestrade and the hapless constable she'd reported the murder to earlier with complete anonymity. *Men.* So utterly predictable when presented with a pretty face and pleasing figure. Whether high- or low-born made no difference; bat an eyelash or smirk salaciously and they become putty in your hands. Shapeless and ready and more than willing to be moulded into whatever your little heart may desire. Whoever said women are the weaker sex had to have been a man. Not that Irene bore a grudge.

She lowered her eyes and walked away. Exhilarated beyond measure that such was the state of affairs, as well as knowing that following hungry eyes swarmed over her retreating backside.

That's right, boys. Looking is free, but I'm not.

Once out of view, Adler turned down a narrow lane. A black suited man approached from the opposite end.

"On time, as usual." He tipped his bowler, face shadowed.

"What news do you have for me?"

"Sherlock Holmes and The Creeper are still at large; Hans Beckert, Dr Mabuse, the Sleepwalker, and a score of the Reich's finest are buried beneath the rubble of Buckingham."

"What about the Minister of the Realm, and the murdered bobbies investigation?"

"Minister Holmes has self-entombed himself at the Diogenes, and Lestrade remains at sea about his dead blue coats."

"Not surprising, he does have a lot on his plate just now. The Gestapo, SS, and SD forces?"

"Those that are left are running about like decapitated chickens, and getting about as far."

Adler snickered. "Anything else?"

"Yes. Our man in 10 Downing Street believes Prime Minister Mosley is considering ordering Martial Law, and King Edward will address the nation this evening."

"Martial Law wouldn't be good for business."

"No, Miss. I've been assured that the PM will be persuaded not to."

"That's a relief. I do look forward to the King's address though; His subjects I'm sure will be reassured by His words."

"Oh, without doubt, Miss."

"We'll talk again." Adler said, then without waiting for a response, turned and walked away. *One, perhaps two more*, she thought, *after all what's chaos without* more *chaos*?

***

Every available empty space on the corkboard in CID was taken by the personnel file and photograph of the three Metropolitan Police Constables murdered in the line of duty: JL Evans, twenty years old; Geoffrey Baker, twenty-three years of age; and a boy at nineteen, Clive Street.

At a glance, the only thing they shared was the proximity of age.

Things were going about as well at another desk across the squad room where Haskins pored over books of photo IDs of women of London near the approximate age of his witness. Lestrade lost count of the times their eyes met and Haskins shook his head returning shoulders slumped in defeat to the book in front of him.

The phone rang, snatched up by Lestrade. "Yes?"

"Dr Michaels, Inspector. A body has just been delivered."

"And?"

"It is the corpse of a German national, Karl Lohmann, of the Berlin Murder Squad."

"So?"

"This may be just a coincidence, sir, but his middle name is Gunther."

"I'll be right down."

Perhaps this was something resembling progress.

"The body was found two blocks away from Buckingham Palace," Dr Michaels reported. "He was in the area when it exploded, I found dust and ash in his hair and on his clothes. Witnesses said they saw him walk a few steps then collapse to the sidewalk."

"How did he die?"

"At first, I thought it was a simple heart attack given his poor physical condition, then I found this. A knife wound here, the blade, wielded by an expert, traversed up through the diaphragm and pierced the heart. Death was nearly instantaneous."

"Did any of the witnesses see who did it?"

"None."

"Send your report up to me the moment you finish the autopsy."

"Of course."

"Leave nothing out, no matter how insignificant or trivial it may appear."

Lestrade ignored Dr Michaels's glare and returned to Haskins and his other headache. He was intercepted at the lift and forced to share it with Tobias Gregson, Special Branch.

"To whom does the Yard owe a visit from Special Branch?"

Gregson stabbed the STOP button, and the lift lurched to a halt. "When the Yard is obviously out of their depth, as has been made all too embarrassingly apparent."

"And they sent *you* to do *what*?"

"Why, bat you cretins out of the way, and steer the Ship of State out of this crisis."

"On whose authority?!"

"Mycroft Holmes, Minister of the Realm. You and your men can make yourselves useful by keeping us fortified with tea, sandwiches, and the like." Then he smiled, disengaged the STOP button, and up they went.

Lestrade always thought Hell was down.

***

"Thank you," I said as the IRA drove us down one street after the other to ensure we were not being followed.

"Don't mention it, lad," the leader replied.

"How is Dylan O'Dan?"

"Recovering slow and painful."

"That's welcome news."

"Aye."

We arrived at the rear of Waterloo Station. Our IRA gunman knew London's back streets better than a native-born cabbie.

"Give him my regards," I called as The Creeper and I exited.

He nodded, grinned like the devil, and drove off.

Below, the gloom emanating from the faces of Dr Watson and Mrs Hudson permeated the air like a virus.

"Inspector Lohmann is dead," Watson said bluntly.

"Knifed on the street in broad daylight," Mrs Hudson added, without emotion.

We mourned privately. There were no tears. None of us had any to give.

"Right," I announced. "The enemy is in disarray. Now's the time to strike."

"Here, here!" my companions cheered.

"You have your assignments. When completed, proceed to the rendezvous."

Without a glance or further word, we separated. The Creeper and I met Wiggins in a damp dark lane. The bricks dripped with condensation.

"Word is Mabuse, Beckert, and most of the Gestapo in London are dead," Wiggins said, joyfully, then more grim, "But so is Inspector Lohmann."

"Go on."

"Mycroft's buried himself in The Diogenes, the guard's been tripled, and there's razor wire strung everywhere. The street's barricaded at both ends with more guards patrolling. Same for Mosley."

"Lestrade?"

"He's been replaced by Gregson and Special Branch."

My eyebrow shot up. Not a surprise, though I thought it would happen too late rather than too soon.

"That's a complication we expected. Be on guard. Special Branch is far more capable and ruthless than Scotland Yard. Off you go."

"See you later!" Wiggins scampered off.

"Good lad," The Creeper observed.

"We've a long night ahead," I replied, and walked away.

The Woman first, then *you,* Mycroft.

***

The nasal high-pitched voice of King Edward VIII blared from speakers mounted on lamp posts and atop Propaganda Ministry vans trolling the streets.

"Loyal subjects, I am speaking to you tonight to assure you in the strongest possible terms that the outrage committed today, as well as the terrorists who perpetrated them, are being handled as I speak. With your continued vigilance, now redoubled, report what you see to Special Branch. Good night. Hail the Empire and the Thousand-Year Reich!"

PC 439 Bertrand Thrall stood at rapt attention, taking in every word spoken by his Sovereign as though they were addressed to him alone. So much so that he didn't hear the footsteps approaching from behind.

Something brushed across his throat, light and quick, like a breath. He tried to swallow, but couldn't. There was blood on his hand, then it was everywhere, flowing out of his throat in bright red sheets. He tried a breath again when the world went black.

"Hell's ready. Hurry now, the Devil doesn't fancy waiting," were the last words he heard, spoken by a *woman*.

***

Irene Adler, *The Woman* responsible for Mary Watson's death inserted the key into her door and was shoved from behind, falling head long and hard to the floor.

I took the key and slammed the door behind us.

She flipped over like a gymnast, a cutthroat razor appearing in her hand.

"*Holmes*! What in the name of Hell," she hissed furiously, then saw my Webley.

"Don't bloody well move," I whispered. "Drop it."

"This little thing? A girl's got to protect herself."

"I won't ask again."

She dropped it, shrugging.

"Kick it over to me."

It clattered across the floor. I observed blood on it, then sent it sliding into the far corner.

"This is new. I like it."

"What are you talking about, woman?"

Adler smiled disarmingly. "*This*. I didn't know you liked the rough stuff."

"What?"

"You were always so polite before. Just to let you know, I like this side of you. So, let's get on with it – unless you want me to take the lead. I'm easy."

In answer, I cocked the hammer back.

Adler raised her eyebrow. "*Fine,* we can *talk* first."

"Sit. I don't have to remind you not to move."

Adler sat, her only sudden move was to primly cross her legs. "Pillow talk *before* and *after.* Throw in cuddling and I'm yours."

"You must have me confused with someone else," I said archly. "There was never pillow talk between us. Or *cuddling.*"

Adler's perfectly shaped brows furrowed together. "You sure?"

I nodded.

"Well, *you* may have all night, but I don't. What do you want to talk about?"

My mind had gone blank. I'd come to avenge Mary. But no words came to mind when faced with this wretched woman.

"Nothing. There's nothing more to be said. The speech I'd planned about your betrayal won't bring Mary back. Nor will it reanimate those policemen you've butchered. Blood's on your hands, and head."

"That's rich, coming from you!" Adler raised her voice, rising only slightly. "We're the same, Sherlock. Alike in every way, including the blood debt we owe. And for the record, I tried to save Mary."

"I don't believe you."

"Don't care if you do. I know in my heart I did everything I could, even if I was too late. For Mary *and* England. As you have. Let me in, I can help."

She was getting to me, and not just with her feminine wiles. Did Adler go too far murdering policemen? Perhaps. But I too had killed in cold blood, and was committed to the murder of my only brother. I jumped into the abyss long ago and I haven't looked back.

I placed my thumb between the hammer and very gently uncocked the pistol.

Adler smiled.

"All right. On two conditions."

"Only two?"

"You are never to be out of my sight, tell me everything you've done and are currently involved in, and with who."

"Sounds like marriage to me," Adler purred. "Not to mention three conditions. Nice try, but I've always been good with numbers."

"Agreed?"

"Agreed, but if that was your best proposal, you'd do better clubbing me on the head and dragging me back to your cave by the hair."

"This is strictly business."

"Whew! In that case, I'll give you another chance."

I handed her the razor. "Let's go. We'll take your car. If I even suspect you're double-crossing me, I won't hesitate to kill you."

"Sheesh! We're not married yet!"

***

Gregson brought in a team of eight and split them into groups of four; the first working the Buckingham Palace attack, the second the incident involving Sherlock Holmes and the Minister of the Realm, the third to provide additional security for the Prime Minister (and of course His Highness), and the fourth tasked with solving the case of the murdered constables.

At first, Lestrade wanted to kill Gregson with his bare hands, then realised he was now free to do as he pleased. And what he pleased was going out, arresting Sherlock Holmes himself, and presenting him in chains to the Minister of the Realm – that would return him to grace, while at the same time getting Gregson off his back for good.

He left Bryan, Haskins, and Hawthorn to serve as Special Branch handmaidens, took Daniels, and quietly left at the first opportunity. He commandeered a car. When necessary, call boxes and City Stations would be used. His first stop was to place Terry in his custody, cuff him, and bring the informant along. The man stopped whining and complaining about how much his light-deprived eyes hurt when Lestrade told him, "There's plenty of places to dump your body if you lie to me. Places you'll rot alone and forgotten *forever.*"

"I swear on my mum and my children, I won't, wouldn't, *ever* lie to you, Inspector."

Lestrade, sitting beside him on the backseat, grinned and pressed the barrel of his service revolver painfully into the informer's ribs. "I don't have all night, and neither do you. Show me all the places you know or have been told Sherlock Holmes has been."

***

The Diogenes was impregnable.

"Forget the Diogenes," Adler said. "The streets in front and around it are bloody fortresses!"

She wasn't wrong; we'd driven the blocks surrounding it scouting for gaps – there weren't any. And even four blocks away, security patrols were thick as maggots on a corpse.

"I don't think the papers you used to get in the first time will work now, Hell, it would take an entire battalion of sappers just to get through the wire; either that or a mortar company. Face it, lover, you missed your chance."

"Oh ye of little faith."

"*Faith?* Since when?!"

"Never. It doesn't require faith to believe in a cause."

"So, what's your plan?"

"I'm working on it. Feel free to contribute anytime."

"I thought my ideas about sappers and a mortar company were pretty good."

"Serious, practical ideas."

"I *was* serious."

"Blueprints!"

"Excuse me?"

"We're going to get the blueprints for this district."

"Why, thinking of building our dream house here?"

"No. If it's impossible to get in from above…"

"Maybe we can get in from below," Adler finished my sentence.

"Precisely!"

"Breaking into the Metropolitan Commission of Sewers will be a breeze."

I turned the car in the right direction. Minutes later, we were in.

"Told ya so!" Adler smirked, irritatingly pleased with herself.

Back at her place, we spread the blueprints out over two tables. Now we had an embarrassment of options; as Mycroft's lodgings in Pall Mall, his official offices in Whitehall, and the Diogenes could all be accessed by the sewer system.

"Best of all," Adler said, "none are guarded!"

"With good reason," I added.

"The '*Great Stink*' revisited!"

"Indeed."

"I'll say this, you know how to show a girl a good time!"

I gave Adler a withering glance.

She threw open a wardrobe, placing one finger under her mouth. "Now, what to wear?"

"Something water-proof, stain-resistant, and oh, rat repelling." I suggested sarcastically.

"I've just the thing!" From deep within her wardrobe, she gathered up two waders, four pairs of knee-high stout rubber boots, and four pairs of rubber gauntlets.

"I'm not going to ask."

Adler smirked. "Wish you would."

"Don't just stand there, get dressed."

As she did, I mapped out our route.

We entered from a lane behind the Carlton Club, turning on our torches when our boots touched down. We'd wrapped several layers of scarves over our noses and mouths, our steps accompanied by squealing schools of rats that scurried along pipes or swam in the foetid water.

"I don't know what I expected, but my imagination didn't come close," Adler said, boot-covered feet stepping widely to avoid coming down on a rat's back.

"We're almost there," I said, employing the footwork of a boxer, wishing The Creeper was here. "There's a turning just ahead."

"And people," Adler noted. "Hello there."

In fact, there were seven people who parted for a man in his early twenties, clean-shaven with black, neatly parted hair and penetrating dark eyes.

"Good evening," he said.

"Good evening to you. We're just passing through, won't trouble you for but a moment," I explained, observing pipes and cricket bats studded with nails in the hands of his companions.

"Pardon me, aren't you Sherlock Holmes?" He chose every word carefully, annunciating with a deliberation and focus common to people who stammer.

"*Sherlock Holmes?! Him?*" Adler snorted uproariously. "He's no more Sherlock Holmes than I am!"

The young man looked deep into my eyes and smiled. I smiled back.

"A pleasure to meet you. I'm Alan Turing."

We shook hands.

"These are my colleagues, fellow intelligentsia both British and German Nazis seek to silence."

"Ladies. Gentlemen." I nodded, making eye contact with each, who put their weapons of mass bludgeoning behind their backs and blushed.

"Nice to meet you," Adler said, pouting. "I'm Irene, Irene Adler."

A kindly woman wearing a deeply saddened expression was brought forward. "Likewise, my dear."

"May I present Mrs Frances Isobel Morcom," Turing said with great affection. "The mother of my late true love Christopher."

I kissed her hand. "Madam, a great pleasure."

"Oh my, *Sherlock Holmes,*" Mrs Morcom exclaimed. "The pleasure is all mine. Christopher was a great admirer, wasn't he, Alan?"

"Indeed he was."

"I am truly honoured." I bowed.

"This is where all of you live?" Adler asked.

"Yes. Here, in the Underground; we move about a lot."

"As do we," I said.

"So, what brings you here? Would I be incorrect in deducing that this particular section of sewer offers you the greatest possible chance of piercing the formidable security measures erected above by your brother, the Minister of the Realm."

"Yes."

"May I show you something?"

"Lead the way."

In a spacious niche was heat, light, and no rats; a black box two metres high with rows of coloured dials sat in the middle of the floor appeared to be the cause.

"Now what – and pardon my French – the bloody hell is *that?*"

"Alan's Oracle, my dear," Mrs Morcom said, giggling into her hand.

"Thank you, Mrs Morcom, but I believe Miss Adler and Mr Holmes require more in the way of an explanation."

"Damn right." Adler stared at the strange contraption, mouth open.

"It is an Oracle, or a Black Box, Miss Adler."

"What does it do?" I chimed in.

"For the past fortnight, nothing it was originally designed for," Turing replied, a confused and explicitly genuine expression of curiosity marking his young face. "Instead, something quite astonishing has happened – the Oracle has transformed this room from a vile sewer branch to this."

"How?"

"When our country went mad, I brought back the inquiries I began at Princeton involving quantum entanglement and reality," Turing said matter-of-factly. "And designed the Oracle to attempt to seek answers to those questions."

"Come again?" Adler's eyes were glazing over.

"Instead of answering hypotheticals with hypotheticals, it has gone a step further," I opined.

"Mr Holmes, The Oracle has taken not one, not thousands, but millions of steps forward. Perhaps more."

"You mean?"

"It has evolved of its own accord," Turing replied with unadulterated fascination.

"Does Professor James Moriarty know of you, or your work?"

Turing shook his head. "I've never met him, but I did read his paper, '*A Treatise Upon The Binomial Theorem,*' as well as his book '*The Dynamics of an Asteroid.*' He doesn't know I'm alive."

"I doubt that."

"If it changed a sewer, could it change the world – or just our nasty little Nazi corner of it?" Adler asked, suddenly alert.

121

"I wish that were so, Miss Adler," Turing said, "alas I strongly suspect *this* to be a simple anomaly; one I expect to reverse itself as incomprehensibly as it occurred."

"Pity, well we must be on our way," I said. "I'm truly sorry Mr Turing and his remarkable machine can't solve our problems. Therefore, *we* must."

"Nice meeting you," Adler called. "Stay safe! Oh, and *Professor,* don't stop fiddling with your black box. Who knows, maybe turning one of those pretty dials this way or that might... Well, it couldn't hurt."

Turing raised both eyebrows. "I'll keep that in mind, Miss Adler."

Some fifteen minutes later, Adler and I stood once again ankle-deep in sludge. By torch light, I checked our position against the blueprints.

"Well?" she asked, feverishly looking around us.

"I didn't know of your aversion to rats."

"Yeah? Well, I didn't know yours either."

I glanced at her.

"Don't think I didn't notice the look on your face, or how you nearly jumped out of your skin back there with that cavalcade of rats."

I quickly looked at the blueprint.

"Thought so. Why don't you just come out and say it? You're terrified of them!"

I ignored her, folding up the blueprint to place in my inside pocket. "We're here."

Adler raised her eyebrow knowingly at me, her lips contorting into a smirk.

I started up the ladder and stopped just under the manhole cover.

"What's the holdup? What are you waiting for? It smells even worse up here!"

"The cavalry," I replied, looking at my watch.

"What cavalry?"

Two explosions, then three, followed by small arms fire erupted.

I quietly lifted and slid the manhole cover to one side, climbed up, and lay flat on the ground. Adler followed suit. We had emerged inside The Diogenes perimeter, and behind the former club itself, near the servant's entrance.

"Who is the cavalry?" Adler whispered, tapping me on the shoulder.

"IRA gunmen," I whispered.

She discreetly let me know the door was locked. "And *how* do you propose we get in?"

"I have a man inside. He'll be here momentarily."

More explosions, this time a little closer, flashed beyond the corner of the building. Machine gun fire increased in intensity.

"For a diversion, your Irish friends sound like they're giving a good accounting of themselves."

"Indeed. I'm not certain they understand the term 'diversion.'"

"Mr Holmes? *Mr Holmes!?*" A quiet voice made itself known in the din.

"Faircloth! I do apologize," I said to the white wild-haired, wrinkled as a prune, but always impeccable manservant. "I didn't hear you."

"Not at all, sir, but I strongly suggest that the young lady and yourself come in quickly," Faircloth replied, unflinching even as explosions and weapons fire sounded around us.

The unassuming thin man was a veteran of Passchendaele, "going over the top" more than any commanding officer on either side; possessing more steel in his frail-appearing frame than Hercules.

"Where's Mycroft?"

"Heavily guarded, sir. I have a secure place where the lady and yourself can wait until the fracas outside has been repulsed, and things relax."

"No offence meant," Adler began, "but why are you helping us?"

"Why, it's quite simple, Miss," Faircloth said, eyes magnified by thick lenses, "I utterly detest the Hun – always have, *always will*."

I'm not one for the supernatural, but the malevolence with which he repeated those last two words chilled the air, as well as myself.

"Uh, yeah," Adler stammered. "Couldn't agree more."

"Please follow me, sir. We shouldn't be standing out in the open, as it were."

Within a few minutes, Adler and I were ensconced in a small library with comfortable leather chairs, coffee, and tea.

"I'll collect you when the coast is clear, sir." Faircloth quietly closed the door.

"Wow," Adler exclaimed. "Doesn't Mycroft know all about Faircloth's hatred of everything German? Hun *and* Nazis?"

"Oh yes, but Faircloth has been with him forever. Mycroft would be lost without him."

Adler took a sip of tea. "How are we going to kill your brother and get out of here alive?"

"Easily, to answer the first part of your question, and Faircloth to answer the second."

"You really are a shit, you know that?"

Do I ever, I thought grimly.

Adler fell into a sullen silence. I checked my wristwatch, and accordingly knew that Dylan O'Dan's lads would be starting to fall back little by little before initiating what would look to Mycroft's men like a panicked retreat, thus, hopefully encouraging them to pursue. Then, it was my show.

And Mycroft's final curtain.

I screwed the silencer to the barrel of my Webley, then put it back into my pocket. Adler, following my lead, did the same.

The door opened.

"It's time, sir," Faircloth announced.

"How goes the fracas?" I asked as we followed the manservant down quiet, empty hallways.

"Well, Mr Holmes, the Minister's security forces are giving chase – a poor tactical decision, if I may be so bold."

"You may. And it is."

Faircloth stopped and smiled widely. "Ah, I see. *Very good.*"

***

Mycroft took a sip of brandy with one hand, while tapping out a tattoo on the desk blotter with the other.

"Very good, thank you Captain," Colonel Wilbert, his Chief of Security, said into the field telephone. "Carry on."

"What's happening?"

"Our Security forces have beaten off the insurrectionists and have taken up pursuit."

"Why?"

"I beg your pardon, Minister?"

"Why have they taken up pursuit?"

"To wipe out the terrorists, to capture, and to interrogate under torture who remains."

"And who precisely is left on guard here?"

Colonel Wilbert puffed out his chest and blew through his other era's grand moustache. "Why, the House Guard and myself, Realm Minister."

Mycroft raised an eyebrow.

"Very good." He took another sip, a bigger one after realising his sarcasm had been wasted on *Colonel Walrus.* "Leave me."

"Sir!" Wilbert blustered, clicked his heels, turned, and marched out, ever-present riding crop tucked under his shoulder.

Tin-plated martinet, Mycroft thought and lit a cigar, *My Kingdom to have Stevens back.*

***

Georg grew more furious by the minute. He'd lost contact with Fine, Cara, and Hawach who should have checked in hours ago following the death of Professor Moriarty. Now, there was no word from Pesch, whom he'd dispatched to the Professor's residence more than fifty-minutes ago. A residence only fifteen-minutes away.

He put on his hat and coat, took a Luger along with his knife and headed out; chastising himself for sending Pesch in the first place.

Two things stood out immediately: one, Hawach was gone along with his car; and two, so was Pesch. *What in the name of Mabuse is going on here,* Georg thought, looking at the unlit brooding building.

His world erupted in pain and light.

Then darkness prevailed.

He awoke arms and legs bound tightly to a chair with a massive headache, face-to-face with the severed heads of Pesch, Hawach, Fine, and Cara staring at him with milk-white eyes.

Someone punched his shoulder. "Look alive, Kraut. He's awake, Professor."

"Turn him round, will you?"

The legs of the chair shrieked like the damned against the stone floor. Slowly the room revolved until an elderly man with rounded shoulders came into view.

"You needn't mourn your accomplices," he said, voice just above a whisper.

"I'm not afraid of you," Georg snarled. "Or death."

The man's head oscillated like a viper about to strike, his expression did not change. No raised eyebrows, a shrug, and his eyes didn't blink, not once as they remained fixed on Georg.

"But you should be," Georg continued defiantly. "Because no one beats Dr Mabuse, *no one*. Not even YOU, Professor Moriarty."

"I've heard he can strike from beyond the grave," Moriarty replied.

"That's right, old man," Georg hissed. "He can, and he will."

"But you can't."

Georg fell silent.

"Turn him back round, Moran, so his dead colleagues can participate in his demise, and welcome him into Death's Domain."

"You're a dead man, Moriarty," Georg screamed. "You're all dead!"

"And Colonel, make it slow and painful."

"Yes, Professor. Been looking forward to this all day."

***

Colonel Wilbert heard the sound of glass breaking, the creak of a window being opened in the Stranger's Room. He cocked his Enfield No Two .38 calibre and moved toward the sound. Pointing the barrel at the middle of the door, he felt a rush of adrenaline he hadn't for decades. He counted to three and threw the door open, feeling like a twenty-year-old again.

A looming monstrosity filled his sight. His gun was snatched from his hand.

"See here," the Colonel yelped when a large hand closed over his mouth. He was picked up and pulled into the room, helpless as a child. The door closed, shutting out the light, leaving him in the dark with a monster.

Lieutenant Hoxton was fed up with old man Wilbert's bluster *and* excessive flatulence. Why, the geezer could barely take a step without breaking wind. In Hoxton's mind, he wasn't even a war hero anymore; those days were *long gone*.

And now the-should-have-retired-a-hundred-years-ago tin soldier couldn't be found.

It was all Hoxton could do not to shout, *Colonel Lard Ass, get off your bum. Wake up!* Instead, he called out, correctly, painfully so:

"Colonel Wilbert, Sir! You're wanted on the phone. Urgent!" He heard an odd cracking sound, like a breaking tree branch. "Colonel? It's Lieutenant Hoxton. You all right, sir?"

A loud thump issued from the Stranger's Room; something heavy falling to the floor.

Hoxton knocked on the door. "Colonel?"

No answer.

He gripped the doorknob, tried to turn it, but it wouldn't budge. A physically strong man, Hoxton gripped it harder, tried again.

Nothing doing.

What the bloody...

131

The door suddenly opened and Hoxton was lifted off his feet. He slammed into the torso of a huge man so hard the wind was knocked out of him. Gasping for air, the lieutenant was picked up and held above in the giant's hands. As though a child, the six-foot Hoxton's muscular body was bent shoulder-to-foot until his spine snapped, then thrown to the floor like an unwanted doll. His last sight in life was the dead eyes of Colonel Wilbert.

The Creeper adjusted his hat, and as though he belonged, strode down the hallways of the Diogenes.

***

Faircloth, Adler, and myself tread the halls carefully, alert to any signs of Mycroft's personal security guard.

"Something's off, Mr Holmes." Faircloth said. "The Diogenes feels empty."

"Empty?" echoed Adler.

"Yes, Miss Adler. Colonel Wilbert, or at least his men, are very efficient and ruthless in the performance of their duties. Particularly Lieutenant's Hoxton and Whitby."

"There's a very good reason for that, Faircloth." I replied.

"May I be permitted to know, sir?"

"Of course, *I* killed them." The Creeper said, emerging from the shadows.

"Son of a bitch," Adler cried out.

Neither Faircloth, nor I were startled.

"Oh, that explains it," Faircloth said calmly. "Thank you, sir."

The wretched woman was still in shock. "How are you so quiet?"

"It's my trade, Miss Adler," The Creeper replied, then turned to address me. "Your brother is alone now."

"At least until the troop returns from its IRA chase."

"They won't be much longer, sir," Faircloth said.

"No. Right. Let's go."

***

"The Diogenes?! Are you mad?!" Lestrade shouted as they pulled up near the bygone club, now fortress.

"I swear, Inspector," Terry replied. "Sherlock Holmes has been here!"

"I say just shoot him, Inspector," Daniels conspired. "He's been leading us by the nose all night."

"I haven't!"

"Shut it," Lestrade snarled. "If that's true, then why bring us here? He knows I wouldn't hesitate to blow his brains

133

out, or better yet – shoot both his knees and leave him for the rats."

"That sounds better," Daniels said enthusiastically. They both talked as though Terry wasn't there.

"It does," Lestrade conceded. "But he'd have to be very stupid to claim the traitor's been here, if he hadn't been. We're here and now I'm curious. Let's have a look."

Daniels shrugged, opening his door.

Lestrade slapped Terry's head hard. "Don't go anywhere."

"We'll be right back," Daniels said.

Terry rattled his cuffs, wondering who the stupid one was.

***

Dr Watson and Mrs Hudson, disguised as Elder Members in the British Union of Fascists, were ushered over the black and white chequerboard floor of the entrance hall of No 10 Downing Street to hear Prime Minister Oswald Mosley speak about the Empire's response to the terrorist bombing of Buckingham Palace. Inside they were joined by Moran, who'd passed many enjoyable hours killing Georg and was primed for more. Hidden on their person was a small amount of plastic explosive which would be discreetly fixed around the podium and audience room as they mingled. Once in place, they would leave shortly before the end of Mosley's remarks, detonating the charges as they drove away, thus decapitating in a stroke the entire upper echelon of British Nazis.

Watson noticed Major General JFC Fuller, William Joyce, and Harold Harmsworth – publisher of the Daily Mail and member of the House of Lords – while Mrs Hudson pointed out David Freeman-Mitford, 2nd Baron Redesdale and member of the House of Lords, as well as his sisters, Lady Diana Mosley and Unity Mitford.

Moran caught their eye and winked lasciviously.

The sound of marching footsteps echoed through the audience chamber like an approaching storm. The assembled guests hushed as I Squad – the elite personal bodyguard of Oswald Mosley – marched in, resplendent in their black fencing jackets, black leather breeches and boots. Eric Piercy, I Squad's moustachioed leader strode in, seeing everyone and everything.

The Mitfords started singing "Comrades the Voices", the anthem of the British Union of Fascists, which was taken up by everyone gathered as Prime Minister Oswald Mosley entered with dramatic flourish through a parting swastika and BUF Flash and Circle Union Banner to thunderous applause.

As the prime minister spoke, Watson, Mrs Hudson, and Colonel Moran set to business with none the wiser.

Except a twenty-four-year-old Hitler aspirant in lederhosen, who'd been watching the three with focus and attention. *What are they up to,* he asked himself. Old geezers, in his experience, didn't split up and move in and out of the guests, occasionally stopping, putting their arms behind their backs and looking around to make sure they weren't caught. He went over to his father, Harry St John Bridger Philby and whispered in his ear.

Moran, the closest to them, heard the man he knew as *Jack* or *Sheikh Abdullah,* comment, "Kim, are you certain?"

The young Philby nodded.

"You'd better tell Eric, then, hadn't you?"

Bloody shite, Moran thought.

As Kim Philby approached Mosley's security chief, Moran started for the exit, making a half-hearted attempt to give Watson and Mrs Hudson the warning signal, all the while feeling *Jack's* eyes all over him.

Dr Watson observed a young man saying something to Eric Piercy, caught just a glimpse of Moran swiftly moving towards the door. *Was that the warning signal?*

Piercy said something to Mosley, who was ushered out of the audience chamber.

It bloody well was!

I Squad took position in front of the dais.

"Ladies and gentlemen," Piercy addressed the crowd, "remain calm, and make your way quickly and quietly to the street."

As he said this, he pointed Mrs Hudson and Watson out to four goons, who moved toward them like hounds to a fox.

Separated and carried along by the crowd, Watson saw one of the blackshirts close on Mrs Hudson. Their eyes met. The lady smiled, took out her detonator, and pressed the button.

Watson did likewise, when a hand gripped his shoulder.

Moran was thrown against the car by two explosions. Windows were blown out, along with bodies. Blood, brick, and glass arced in the air suddenly ablaze. Ears ringing and disoriented, he pulled himself together, got in, and pulled away. At the end of the street, Moran pressed the button on his detonator. Dr Watson and Mrs Hudson did their part; he saluted them.

A fireball blossomed, blowing the door like petals, along with the twisted deadly thorns of the wrought iron fence clanging into the middle of Downing Street.

Screams filled the air.

They serenaded tone deaf Sebastian Moran as he sped away.

***

As we neared Mycroft's suite of offices, we heard men screaming and groaning.

"They're bringing the wounded into the front parlour," Faircloth said.

The sirens of ambulances and fire trucks also filled the air, along with the oppressive odour of cordite.

"We must move quickly, sir."

The four of us ducked down and went past the chaos beyond the open French doors, then turned unobserved down the hallway leading deeper into The Diogenes. Closer to Mycroft, ensconced in his Ninth Circle of Hell.

Treachery.

As we turned into the hallway leading to my brother's inner sanctum, so did Lieutenant Hart and Inspector Lestrade and another man. The six of us stopped and stared at each other as though transformed into statues. The Creeper threw himself in front of us as Lestrade, Hart, and the other man I recognised as Inspector Daniels drew their pistols. Adler and I drew ours.

The Creeper lunged forward, took hold of Daniels and Hart, smashing them against Lestrade. A muffled pistol shot was heard among grunts of pain. A bullet erupted from the side of The Creeper enveloped in a cloud of blood, narrowly missing me, burying itself in the wall.

Daniels, Hart, and Lestrade lay in an unconscious pile.

The Creeper staggered back a step.

"You all right?" Adler inquired.

He checked himself before sitting heavily on the floor. "Yes, Miss Adler. Looks like it went right through."

Faircloth rushed to his side and stuffed the wounds front and back with linen doilies to staunch the blood. "Go on, Mr Holmes. I'll see to our friend."

Adler and I exchanged a glance.

"Ready?"

"More than ready." Adler smiled, drawing back the hammer of her pistol.

That reminded me never to turn my back on *The Woman* ever. It was the same smile that murdered four policemen in cold blood just for being policemen.

We entered Mycroft's outer office. His secretary, a very young man, quite out of his depth, obliged us by having his back turned while talking on the phone:

"Yes, Inspector Gregson. Of course, sir. I'll inform the Minister of the Realm at once."

He found the barrel of my pistol pressed against his head.

"Not a sound, pretty boy," Adler said, her index finger pressed against her red lips.

I directed him to have a seat with a wave of my gun.

"Is the Minister of the Realm in?" Adler asked. "Nod once for yes, twice for no."

He nodded two times.

"Oh, that's *inconvenient,*" she rolled her eyes, putting on her best pout. "We simply *must* see him."

"What did Inspector Gregson want?" I asked.

"*Whisper,*" Adler said menacingly, emphasising her point with her razor.

The man's eyes darted between Adler and myself many times before frantically shaking his head *No*.

"No matter," I said. "Mycroft will tell me everything I want to know. We're brothers."

Faircloth came in, along with The Creeper.

"You all right?"

"Much better, Mr Holmes, thanks for asking. Mr Faircloth here informed me that at one point in the Great War he served as a field medic – a very good one," The Creeper said.

"Why, it's just like riding a bicycle." Faircloth blushed. "Once you've done it, you never forget."

"We put Lieutenant Hart and Inspector's Lestrade and Daniels into separate rooms, bound and gagged. Mr Faircloth locked them in."

I nodded. "When we came in, the young man was on the phone with Inspector Gregson. Stand watch in case the man from Special Branch shows up."

"Will do." The Creeper and Faircloth said as one, then grinned at each other like mismatched mates.

I reached across the desk, and buzzed Adler and I in.

When Mycroft saw us, he didn't so much as raise an eyebrow.

"Brother! Miss Adler, good to see you again! Brandy?"

I scanned the room quickly for anything out of place.

The Woman was perplexed. "You were expecting us?"

"Why, of course, Miss Adler," Mycroft replied jovially.

"Are you drunk?" I asked.

"Not a bit." My brother reignited the cigar he retrieved from the edge of a crystal ashtray, sitting quite at ease. "Come now, it doesn't take a feat of deductive genius to know you'd make another attempt. That doesn't mean we can't be civil."

"No," I said, aiming my pistol at his head. "Any last words?"

***

"Are they dead?"

"I would expect so, Professor." Moran replied, lighting a cigar. He poured himself a generous whiskey, took a sip, and noticed Moriarty gazing sphinx-like into space. "Professor?"

"Leave me."

Moran grabbed his glass, stuck the cigar in his mouth, and left. Still waters run deep and dark when Professor James Moriarty transformed into stone.

The crime genius picked up the phone. "Number 10, retrieve and recover."

***

For hours, from opposite ends of Downing Street, Wiggins and Simpson watched as the injured and the dead were carried from the smouldering ruin, but they couldn't get close enough to catch sight of Dr Watson or Mrs Hudson. Even as night began to fall, the street was too closely guarded; not to mention sealed off. Maybe they were all right, maybe they weren't.

Wiggins frowned. He and Simpson confirmed that they'd seen a lot of blood. As well as arms, legs, and other body parts. Things they'd rather not have seen.

***

"Check the hospitals," Professor Moriarty said into the phone. "*Find them.*"

"Is there anything I can do, Professor?" Inspector Tobias Gregson of Special Branch asked as he entered unannounced. "I couldn't help overhearing."

"You'd be wise *not* to *overhear* in future, Inspector. Or enter my presence unannounced. How did you get in here?"

Gregson smiled winningly as he flashed his ID and sidearm.

"That Special Branch badge will only get you so far, Gregson. It will not work here again."

"Is that a threat?"

"Without doubt," Moriarty stared him down with deeply sunken eyes, cold as marble, black as obsidian.

"That's why we get along so well," Gregson said, affably. "We understand one another intimately. If only the rest of the world did the same. We'd be so much better for it."

"What do you want? If you're here to eavesdrop – I mean *overhear* – then you've wasted your time, and more importantly, *mine.*"

Still smiling, Gregson took a chair. "Word my people have is that Prime Minister Mosley died, along with his wife Diana Mitford, her sister Unity, and a who's who of British fascists. Seems that for now at least, Minister of the Realm Holmes rules Nazi England."

"That's gratifying. Have you spoken to the Realm Minister?"

144

"I was on my way to inform him of the situation, when I heard the Diogenes was under attack by Irish Republican Army terrorists."

"I hope all is well."

"It appears they've been run off by Realm Minister Holmes' security detachment, Professor. If there's nothing else, I'll be on my way."

"Good evening." Moriarty turned round in his chair.

"Evening, Professor."

Your days are coming to an end, old man; much sooner than you anticipate, Gregson thought, extremely satisfied the plan for his future was coming to fruition.

***

Watson hoped he was dead. Or that he soon would be. The pain he felt was excruciating, ameliorated barely by the morphia he was being given. He dreaded consciousness. At least unconscious, he was able to spend time with his Mary in a kind of phantasm. She held him, cradling his head on her lap.

"It is all right, John," she said soothingly.

He so longed to join her.

"How is he, Rotwang," Mary asked, jolting him in a Frenchman's voice.

"Agitated, thanks to you," a German-accented voice replied.

"Well?" The Frenchman's face was hidden by a black hood.

"I've repaired most of the burns and blast damage to his shoulders and back, however, full healing will take much time."

"What about the woman?"

"She was much closer to the explosion; she is now comatose. I doubt she will survive."

"What is that contraption and the purpose of the wires attached to her head?"

"A device of my own invention; you wouldn't understand."

"You'll do everything you can, however."

"Of course. The next twenty-four hours will tell the tale."

Oh, poor Mrs Hudson, was Watson's morphine-blurred last thought before losing consciousness.

***

"Professor Moriarty, as I've explained, Dr Watson and Mrs Hudson *were not there.*"

The Professor nodded; the massively bearded Aboriginal tracker – Dick-a-Dick or King Richard as he's been called – was eminently qualified. That was why Moriarty hired him.

"However, I know where they are."

"Do go on, Jungunjinanuke."

"They were taken by clever, but clumsy men to a haunt in Limehouse," the Aborigine replied and bowed, impressed and grateful that the Englishman took the time and addressed him by his native name. Something unheard of, as English Imperialists never respect other cultures.

"Very good. Formulate a plan, extricate the Good Doctor and Mrs Hudson, and bring them to me."

"It will be done tonight."

***

The figurative chasm between Mycroft and I grew into a literal abyss in the few seconds between taking aim and pulling the trigger, when the cold metal of a gun barrel dug into the back of my head like an ice pick, cold and sharp.

"Drop it."

"Ah, Inspector Gregson," Mycroft exclaimed. "What a pleasant surprise! Do come in. Brandy?"

As instructed, I dropped my gun. My head exploded in red-coloured pain before everything went black. Just like the Nazi flag.

Sometime later, I came to.

"Well, this is a disappointment," Mycroft's voice was oddly distorted no doubt due to my cracked skull. "You woke up."

Naturally, I was bound to a chair.

The room was spinning.

"Why can't you just die?!"

I smiled at my brother and vomited. It spattered on the floor and Mycroft's desk.

He stood up quickly – in fact, faster than I'd ever seen him move ever.

"Disgusting pig," Gregson shouted from my left.

"No, Gregson," Mycroft yelled as I doubled over in the chair, dry retching.

"Why don't I just execute the traitor here and now," Gregson insisted, punching my arm.

"Because *I am* the Minister of the Realm. Get Faircloth in here and clean him up! He will die tonight, in public!"

"You really don't know when to quit, do you?" Adler whispered into my ear.

It hurt just to move my eyes sideways. "You know me."

"All too well."

"Step away from him, Miss Adler," Mycroft threatened. "Unless you wish to join him."

"Switching sides wouldn't be the smart play, Irene," Gregson moved in, taking her by the arm. "After all you've done."

"Who said I was switching sides?"

"I saw the look in your eye," Gregson replied. "Forget it. *He'll* never forget or forgive what you've done, *all those innocent policemen!*"

"He's right," I croaked to her, voice hoarse. "You chose your course."

Then I passed out.

***

Jungunjinanuke accompanied by his mates, Jerry and Fred, watched the lightless warehouse like a dingo stalking prey. The Thames could be heard lapping at the shore in the darkness beyond, *"The Limehouse Blues"* which echoed

Gertrude Lawrence's voice, haunting and spectral, from pubs over the cobblestones.

All day Jungunjinanuke moved in two worlds; the real, and a waking dream that showed him this place, and the doom awaiting him within. Now the real world, and his dream had become one.

"Right mates," he said in their native Wergaia language, slipping on his Kurdaicha shoes, which were said to leave no footprints, rendering the wearer silent and invisible.

They were all *Featherfoots,* sorcerers of their Wotjobaluk tribe; each carried the seven-inch bone of a dead man, which was imbued with powerful magic, sharpened at the end so that when pointed at anyone who got in their way they would die instantly. Jungunjinanuke squared his broad shoulders and fearlessly stepped first into the shadows he welcomed. Rats skittered behind the walls, accompanied by the electric whine of a machine. As the whine grew louder, the odour of ozone filled the air as the three Featherfoots made their way down the dark corridor, the plaster walls cracked and blooming with mould. Light beams from the street eerily crisscrossed the hall at intervals from the warehouse's high windows.

Same as my dream, Jungunjinanuke thought.

A kettle shrieked, its ear-piercing whistle lanced through the dark corridor like a scalpel from one of many dark doorways opening onto empty vast rooms. Just ahead a dull yellow light streamed from one of those open doors.

The kettle continued its banshee scream.

Isn't anyone going to get that, Jungunjinanuke thought, waving his mates forward.

Then someone did.

They'd reached the open doorway. Jungunjinanuke lay on the floor, and looked in.

His blood ran cold.

A man with wild hair was leaning over a woman strapped to a metal table, whispering into her ear and stroking her hair with his metal hand. The woman had silver tubing inserted into her temples; her eyes were open, staring into the vaulted ceiling's darkness.

On another table lay a man, similarly restrained; also unconscious.

They must be Dr Watson and Mrs Hudson, thought Jungunjinanuke grimly as he stood.

Jerry and Fred saw the strange tableau too.

151

Just how are we going to get them out of here, Jerry asked using sign language.

I do not know, Jungunjinanuke signed back.

Let's start with Mr Metal Hand, Fred suggested, taking out his pointing bone.

Jungunjinanuke nodded, and thus silently, the tribal sorcerers entered.

Mr Metal Hand was oblivious to their presence. The way he whispered into Mrs Hudson's ear was indecent to Jungunjinanuke's mind. He, Fred, and Jerry crouched down and pointed their sharpened bones at the strange wild-eyed man. Fred grunted as he was suddenly thrown to the floor, his head hitting it hard and bouncing up like a rock.

"What have we here, Beadle," an old woman spoke, holding a small calibre pistol to Jerry's head; its grip could also be used as brass knuckles. Her eyes were black as night and hard as iron.

"Common thieves, Mother Toulouche," the stout barrel-chested, ape-like man replied as he threw Jerry to the floor; both Australians lay still.

"Do not move," Mother Toulouche said, turning her *Apache* revolver on Jungunjinanuke.

"Drop that," Beadle ordered. "What is *it?* It looks like a *bone,* I've never seen anything like that, have you Mother?"

"I have not, odd looking buggers, ain't they?"

"Get those untermensch out of here," Rotwang shouted, waving his metal hand. "Kill them outside! Or they'll contaminate this entire area!"

"We don't take orders from you," Mother Toulouche shouted back. She pointed the barrel-less revolver at Jungunjinanuke's head. "We kill who we want, where we want!"

Glass broke, the muffled report of a rifle shot could be heard. Mother Toulouche's eyes widened in astonishment as a small red hole opened between them. Then the man named Beadle met the same fate.

***

Rotwang gaped as both crumpled dead to the floor, then stared as a giant bearded man filled the door. He was joined by a tall, thin man wearing a trimmed goatee, a high-powered Savage Model 19 rifle with a Lyman 438 field scope slung about his shoulder, pointing a Luger pistol at Rotwang.

"I quite agree, Ivan," the urbane man dressed in black from neck to feet said, fixing a monocle to his left eye, giving it a monstrously large appearance. *"Germans!"*

He aimed and fired.

The bullet struck Rotwang squarely in the centre of his throat. The metal fingers of his artificial hand flexed convulsively as the German scientist tried and failed to breathe. He was dead before his body hit the floor.

***

"You needn't fear us, my friend. I am Count Zaroff and this is Ivan," the hunter addressed to Jungunjinanuke, caressing a livid deep scar that disfigured his high forehead. "Professor Moriarty is a man after my own heart; he always has a contingency plan in place. Now, let's get Dr Watson, Mrs Hudson, and your men to safety *quickly*. I'm expecting guests to arrive on my island soon."

***

I regained consciousness and found myself in a straitjacket shackled to a metal bar in the window-less back of a police van. *The Creeper and Faircloth must be dead,* I thought, *two more lives Mycroft must pay for.*

A metal slide opened.

"Thought you'd be awake," Gregson said jovially. "Just between you and I, your brother may want you gone quickly, but I want you to die *slowly;* either at the end of a rope, or in a gas chamber."

"I doubt you'll get your wish, Gregson. Unless you plan on killing Mycroft yourself. Don't tell me you haven't thought about it."

"Keep your traitor's mouth shut! I thought no such thing!"

"You don't have to admit anything, Gregson. I'm certain Mycroft and his agents have kept a close eye on you."

Gregson slammed the slide shut.

Alone at last, I began working to free myself when I heard shots. The windscreen exploded. The police van veered sharply to the left, then came to a metal crunching halt. I slammed against the bare metal side hard, dislocating my shoulder. Not the way I would've chosen, but it made it easier to free myself from the strait jacket.

The back doors swung open to reveal Sebastian Moran.

"Are you going to sit in there all night?"

I grimaced. I threw down the straitjacket, then popped my shoulder back into its socket.

"Bloody Christ all mighty," Moran exclaimed. "I didn't need to see that!"

"And I didn't know you were so squeamish, Colonel." I exited the police van. "Where's Mycroft?"

"He lit out of here the moment we started shooting, but I hit his engine and disabled his radio. He'll not get far."

"What are we waiting for?"

"You."

"Let's go."

True to Moran's word, Mycroft's limousine sat nearby, smoke pouring from beneath the bonnet. His security detail surrounded the vehicle brandishing Sten submachine guns which they fired as soon as we turned the corner. Concrete and brick exploded around us.

Before I took cover, I saw Mycroft's enormous silhouette in the back seat.

"Those four men are all your brother has," Moran said.

"Right. Take a position in this building, preferably an upper storey window? In case more of his goons come looking for him."

"Watch over you, like an angel?" Moran smirked and turned toward the building.

"No, like a man who hits what he shoots at," I called after him.

With us were three gunmen I didn't know. Each carried an American Thompson machine gun; one handed me an American Colt M1911 pistol. I nodded my thanks. He asked if I wanted a grenade, to which I replied with an enthusiastic nod. On the count of three each of us released the pin and rolled our Mk 2 grenades over the pavement, while the fourth man emptied his "Tommy" gun at Mycroft's men.

The explosions shattered the surrounding building's windows, then fell an eerie silence.

I cautiously peeked around the corner of the building. Mycroft's security detail lay on the pavement, while Mycroft remained unscathed in his armour-plated – though bullet-riddled – car. I walked up to the passenger door and tapped on the window with the barrel of my gun.

Unfazed, my brother looked at his watch as though this was any ordinary day.

I suppose the day you die would be *any ordinary day,* I thought.

"Open the door."

Mycroft lit a cigar instead.

"Stubborn, isn't he?" Moran appeared beside me.

"Always," I replied. "He can't be compelled, and we don't have a six-pound anti tank gun at our disposal."

"So, we wait for him to finish his cigar, get hungry, what?"

"No, we tow him to a secure location."

Moran nodded and motioned to his men, who moved our car into position. Once joined by a stout chain, we slowly pulled Mycroft's car down the street.

My brother in chains. That's more like it, I thought.

A sound akin to a giant insect buzzed around us. Suddenly we were illuminated in a circle of blinding light.

"There!"

I looked. A Sikorsky R4 helicopter dropped to street level and hovered, blocking our path, its searchlight bright as the sun. I leaned out of my window and shot it out, plunging us into sudden darkness.

"Down," Moran shouted.

I threw myself to the floor, colliding with him, as the roar of machine guns competed with the shower of hot blood and glass shards raining down from where a few seconds before stood his men and the windscreen.

Moran returned fire. I dove out of the car and shot at the muzzle flashes coming from the right side of the helicopter. The helicopter paused its onslaught. Best case the shooters were dead; worst case they were reloading.

"Move," Moran yelled again.

We ran into a twisted narrow lane; men shouting, sounds of pursuit close behind, so close I swore I could hear soldiers breathing, their jackboots hammering the pavement.

"Follow me." I elbowed Moran out of the way; every turn and dead-end of London's back-lane labyrinth flashed in my mind's-eye. "And keep up, or I'll leave you behind!"

"Oy, do you even have your bloody eyes open?!"

I didn't, there was no need to.

I smiled, hearing Moran grunt in pain as he collided with a brick wall.

We arrived at length at a safe house known only to myself.

"That was a right bloody cock-up, and no mistake."

Sirens wailed past the building we hid in.

"Where are Watson and Mrs. Hudson?" I panted.

"Haven't the foggiest. They're on their own," Moran breathed out.

I nodded.

"I'm not waiting." He rose to his feet. "By now they're dead, or in the hands of the Gestapo. See you in hell, Sherlock Holmes."

"Stop or I will kill you where you stand. Hands where I can see them."

"What is this? A double cross?"

"Where are Watson and Mrs Hudson, Colonel? I won't ask again."

"I told you I don't know! Last time I saw them was at 10 Downing Street. We placed the charges, Mosley's security found us out; Watson and Mrs Hudson detonated theirs, as did I."

"I talked to Wiggins and Simpson. They told me *you* were outside, safe, when the place exploded. You got in the car, detonated *your* charge and drove away. *You left them behind!*"

"What could I have done?"

"Where are they?"

"The Professor sent people to retrieve them. He didn't take me into his confidence."

"I wonder why."

"You wouldn't, if you knew Moriarty."

"I'll be visiting him soon. Tell the Professor that Watson and Mrs Hudson better be in good health when I get there."

"Tell him yourself," Moran replied, looking out a grime-covered window.

He slipped out without another word.

I will, I thought, slipping the gun back in my pocket.

***

I entered Moriarty's abode without a sound.

From rooms directly ahead, I could hear chanting.

I moved cautiously and quietly, the pistol a reassuring presence and weight in my hand.

What the devil?!

A half-naked trio of Australian Aborigines shuffled back and forth, waving feathers and chanting over the unmoving forms of Watson and Mrs Hudson.

"Stop where you are," I commanded, entering the room.

"Oh, do be still," Moriarty said, emerging from the shadows to stand between us. "May I present Jungunjinanuke and his friends, Fred and Jerry. My apologies, gentlemen, I do not know your *real* names."

The heavily bearded, muscular natives of the Australian Continent paid neither Moriarty nor myself any attention, continuing their ministrations as though we were not even there.

To my astonishment Watson and Mrs Hudson both appeared alert and well, despite their dreadful pallor. On closer inspection, Mrs Hudson had small holes at her temples as though something had been inserted.

"You see," Moriarty said. "They are well on their way to a full recovery."

"What happened to them?"

Moriarty stroked his clean-shaven chin. "They had been removed from the rubble of 10 Downing Street by agents in the employ of a Frenchman, taken to a warehouse in Limehouse, and – for want of a better term – experimented upon. Especially Mrs Hudson."

My blood boiled. "*Where* exactly is this warehouse?"

"So predictable," Moriarty tsked at me. "Always ready for gunplay and fisticuffs, spoiling for it in fact; you have more in common with Moran than you know."

I glared at him.

"Their captors have already been dealt with, Holmes. They are quite dead."

"Who were they?"

"Nobodies, really. The Frenchman Fantomas, two of his gang, and a German scientist of ill repute named Rotwang."

I'd heard of The Fantomas and Rotwang - neither could be considered a *nobody*. "Fantomas is dead?"

"My agents are still investigating, however, two of his gang and Rotwang's deaths have been confirmed."

I raised my eyebrow.

"I held up my end of our bargain. Dr Watson and Mrs Hudson are safe."

"Mycroft lives still. I'm going after him."

"Again? Your plan to decapitate the government has succeeded. Mosley, Mabuse, Beckert, as well as the aristocrats instrumental in handing over England to the Nazis, are dead. If you never take my advice again, heed me now. Regroup, recoup. Mycroft has nowhere to go. He is Minister of a shattered Realm, reduced to a stationary target – always in your crosshairs."

I ignored him and went to Watson's side. He favoured me with a wink. I placed my hand gently on his shoulder, holding it there for only a few seconds, then moved on to Mrs Hudson. She smiled. I touched my temple and in reply, my landlady gave me a don't-you-worry-about-me shrug and placed her hand over mine.

Without a word, I left.

***

The streets of London echoed with sirens.

"Stay in your homes! This is a national emergency! Any person found on the Street will be arrested!"

The message blared stridently from street-corner government loudspeakers.

Moriarty was right, logic told me that. Except I'd abandoned logic long ago. Now hatred animated me; possessed me whole and entire. I found solace in its grip. It gave me the strength to go on.

A police car approached, searchlight sweeping over doorways, flashing off shuttered windows. I ducked into an alley, waiting impatiently for it to pass. The car stopped in front of the alley's entrance. The searchlight penetrated only a few feet into the shadows, its cone of illumination well away from me.

"Search the lane," Lestrade shouted, service revolver in his hand.

Doors slammed closed, torchlight blazed into the alley in front of half a dozen policemen, stripping away darkness with every sweep.

With a flick of my wrist and a whisper, my self-made spring-loaded fighting baton extended.

"There he is!"

"Stop where you are! Don't move!"

The lane was narrow, allowing only two of London's finest to approach me directly while blocking their fellow officers with their bodies. This gave me the advantage.

"Hands up!" A pencil-moustached pretty boy waved his torch about, its light bouncing off the brick walls and myself like a deranged sprite.

"Cuff him," Lestrade shouted from the back of the group. "Stop playing about!"

I stepped forward in an *Avant* front lunge. Pretty Boy's eyes widened as he watched his torch go spinning in the air. Then, I crouched down into a *Grenoville* or frog stance and proceeded to break his wrist, then striking his calf hard. He screamed and crashed hard to the cobbles, writhing in pain.

"Blithering idiot!" The man next to him charged.

My baton struck his forehead dead centre; he was probably dead as his body fell back into the men rushing forward.

All Hell broke loose.

My expertise at *canne de combat* was too much for them as I laid out the following two men in quick succession. That left Lestrade and another man.

"Don't just stand there," the Inspector yelled. "Shoot him!"

The man – more a lad – looked at the pile of dead or unconscious men at his feet, then at me; his eyes wild and darting.

"Don't think! *Shoot!*"

The boy hesitated just long enough. I attacked. A flash blinded me. Just then a shot rang out, deafening in the close quarters of the lane.

The boy opened his mouth and blood poured out. He gulped, bringing up more that ran down his chin. His brows furrowed together. He looked at me in shock and confusion. As his knees gave out, he sank quietly to the pavement. Lestrade killed his own man.

"*Traitor,*" Lestrade hissed, his gun pointing at me.

I threw my baton. I watched it spin in slow motion through the air. Lestrade saw it too, his eyes widening, crossing as the weighted close combat weapon made bone cracking contact with his head.

Muzzle flash bright and blinding, gun boomed...

In one fluid motion, I ducked and moved to the right, my eyes tracking the bullet as it tumbled and seared the air, a fiery blunt object. Fueled solely by instinct I fled. Lestrade fell crashing to the pavement. Angel Court blurred around me, as though I was underwater. Blurred images of brick and windows clung to me like cobwebs.

I drove on until I stood, breathing heavily, cloaked in shadows across from Mycroft's Pall Mall residence. One man guarded the front entrance. I bypassed him and went to the servant's door where Faircloth was keeping watch. He let me in. I was overjoyed to find him alive.

"This way, sir," he escorted me to the study.

I opened the door. The room was empty.

"Forgive me, sir," Faircloth said calmly.

"WHERE *IS* HE?!" I roared.

"Mycroft is alive and well, but pumped so full of amobarbital he doesn't know what planet he's on."

"I didn't ask how he was, Faircloth. I asked *where!*"

"Currently, the former Realm Minister is in the custody of the American OSS and is being transported somewhere he can do England no further harm."

I gaped at the frail looking man.

"Will there be anything else, sir?"

"You're a wonder, Faircloth! No, nothing else, but do keep in touch."

"Of course, sir. And congratulations."

END